"You are a scheming, ruthless man, McKay."

Cort just grinned back at her from across the kitchen table. "Cruel," he said. "I'd be completely dashed now if I didn't know you admired some of my qualities."

"What conceit!" Abby protested. As she reached up to the cupboard for sugar, Cort's hand closed about her wrist, filling Abby with longing. Here was a man who fascinated her—annoyed her—a man whose tough physical appeal and gentle touch melted her insides. If only he wasn't hell-bent on protecting his business interests.

"You'll do anything to protect that damned island development of yours, won't you?" *And I,* she thought suddenly, *could easily fall in with your plans.*

Cort stood up, hands on hips. "Why so offended? You're a beautiful woman—I'm a normal man. I'd like to get to know you. I'd like to make love to you...."

Australian author **ANN CHARLTON** traces the beginning of her writing to a childhood period when, in trying to avoid nightmares, she began telling herself a story, continued each night. Her professional writing began with a short-story contest. Now, she writes every weekday, interspersed with looking after her family. Tennis, sketching, reading, modern music and dancing are other interests. When both daughters have finished high school, Ann looks forward to travel and seeing new places.

Books by Ann Charlton

HARLEQUIN PRESENTS
857—AN IRRESISTIBLE FORCE

HARLEQUIN ROMANCE
2660—A PLACE OF WILD HONEY
2684—NO LAST SONG
2701—WINTER SUN, SUMMER RAIN
2762—THE DRIFTWOOD DRAGON

These books may be available at your local bookseller.

ANN CHARLTON

titan's woman

Harlequin Books

TORONTO • NEW YORK • LONDON
AMSTERDAM • PARIS • SYDNEY • HAMBURG
STOCKHOLM • ATHENS • TOKYO • MILAN

Harlequin Presents first edition September 1986
ISBN 0-373-10912-1

Original hardcover edition published in 1986
by Mills & Boon Limited

CHAPTER ONE

CORT McKAY strode through his outer office, a frown on his face and a hard hat bearing the name TITAN in his hand. Marlene felt the change even before she looked up. The quiet office charged with energy as he passed her desk. Her dried flower arrangement trembled.

'Coffee, Marlene, please,' he said brusquely as he went into his own office. Marlene sat for a moment, grimacing—waiting for Cort's reaction to the news clipping she'd put on his desk.

'Oh hell!'

There it was. She winced and hurried to fetch his coffee. Not a good day so far. Judging by his frown, all was not well on the North City building site yet. Even Cort's personal intervention hadn't persuaded the unions to lift their ban yet, and the job was running way behind the completion date. As Chairman and Managing Director of TITAN he had no need to become involved with matters at that level. In fact, Marlene thought, remembering the long faces of the G.M. and Projects Manager, he'd probably put a few noses out of joint by doing so. But Cort controlled his own company—had built it up from an ailing infant to the construction giant worthy of its name and he was no figurehead.

'Damnation!' he burst out as she took the coffee into his office. He tossed the news clipping down in disgust. 'That bunch of women again—haven't they got anything better to do than march around with placards? Two strikes in the last three months, two

5

demonstrations by this crowd and now they plan to
march in here—' he grumbled. 'I keep expecting to
hear any minute that Spalvins is buying up TITAN
shares——'

'Even Adelaide Steamship might find a TITAN
takeover more than they could handle,' Marlene
smiled.

He grunted. 'We're safe enough at the moment I
suppose. Who is this—Abigail Milburn? She seems to
be spokesman for A.W.E.'

'Spokesperson,' she corrected. 'Aware Women for
the Environment it stands for. I don't recognise her
name, Cort, but Dave might have met her when they
demonstrated about that old church on the Grady Hill
site——'

'The old church *foundations* you mean,' he said
drily. 'We had to cordon the whole damned thing off
and stop work all because of a few convict bricks in the
ground——' He glanced up at her. 'Don't get me
wrong—I just love the idea of preserving the past of
this great country but I wish history hadn't left its
mark on our site.'

'What will you do about that, Cort?'

'Don't know yet. We might be able to turn it to
advantage——'

Marlene was interested to know how he would do
that. The Grady Hill job was a suburban shopping
complex designed along TITAN's tried and tested
lines, and fifteen percent of the project was already
pre-committed. The foundations were smack in the
middle of the planned building.

He swiped up the news clipping with one big hand,
read it again.

'Damn, damn—the last thing I want is a group of
environment nuts nosing around——'

'They only want to save those old trees on the

Winston site this time—according to the paper. That's why they're coming here.'

'Hmmm. According to the paper.' Cort's light blue eyes flicked up at her. It was like a buzz of electricity. Marlene never got used to it. 'Better get Dave in—and you can sit in on this, too, Marlene——'

Marlene went out and buzzed Dave Sinclair's office. She knew what was bothering Cort. It was Paradise Island. He could just about take the delay on completion of North City and he could swallow, albeit bitterly, the delay in commencement at Grady Hill or Winston but he wouldn't tolerate any interference with his plans for Paradise. He had played the entrepreneur before on a small scale but the resort for Paradise Island—that was his baby. And Cort had something to hide. It made him nervous having an environment group paying such close attention to TITAN just now when he had his financial backers lined up and the project close to starting. Those backers were a highly-strung bunch though—happy to be in the race if there was profit to be had quickly and cleanly, but they would bolt through the barriers at the first hint of the delays that a vociferous environment lobby could cause.

Dave Sinclair, briefed by Marlene, followed her into Cort's office. He was another cause for the occasional long face among the more conservative of the TITAN executive. Dave was a troubleshooter—he investigated and negotiated wherever Cort's instinct told him there was need for investigation and negotiation. He reported directly to Cort—a very unusual circumstance, the conservatives muttered among themselves. But Cort was a very unusual man.

'Morning, Cort. Nice day for a demonstration.' Dave grinned as he sat down.

Lightning-blue eyes flicked up at him. 'Watch it, or

I'll hightail it out of here and leave you to face A.W.E.
and Ms Milburn alone.'

Dave held up his hands in mock terror. 'No boss,
no. Not that. I'd rather face a pack of starving dingoes
than a crowd of idealistic women. It took a lot of moral
fibre to front up to them.'

'Did you meet this Abigail Milburn at the Grady
Hill fiasco?' Marlene asked.

'Didn't I tell you? A great big hulking woman—she
looked as if she should be working on one of those oil
rigs in Bass Strait. All yellow plastic and stringy hair.
It was raining . . . I thought at one stage she was going
to hit me,' he added with a reminiscent shudder.

'Why so craven?' Marlene mocked. 'A big strapping
lad like you.'

'You had to be there—some of those ladies were
built like bulldozers and as for Ms Milburn—I swear
she was as formidable as you, Cort.'

Marlene laughed. Cort was six foot four and built
on a magnificent scale. No fat, not even now when he
spent so much time at a desk. Muscle and plenty of it.
There wasn't a man she knew who measured up to
Cort—not even her own Charlie whose physique had
grown comfortably in their years of marriage—so
there was little chance of finding a woman to compare
with him.

'Hmmm. Maybe I'd better see them myself when they
march in here. I doubt Nicholsen or the others would
object to me butting in on *this* job,' Cort said wryly.

'You're going to *let* them march in here?'

'Can't see how we can do anything else. After their
unfortunate clash with our site crew yesterday,
TITAN might look like a bully if we refuse to let
them in to make their complaints.' But his eyes
narrowed and he turned the news cutting over and
over in his hands. Dave shrewdly studied his boss.

'They couldn't know anything about Paradise, Cort, if that's what's on your mind. Their group is primarily concerned with the city environment.'

Cort grunted. 'Let's assume that anyway. When they arrive, see if you can cut this Milburn woman out from the herd and get her in here. I'm damned if I'll waste my time talking to a shrieking mob.'

'Better you than me Cort. I wish you luck with the bulldozer breed. The women you're accustomed to aren't in the A.W.E. mould.'

Marlene frowned, feeling a sneaking sisterly sympathy for the women who disapproved of her employers.

'Generalising again, Dave. And what, pray, do you consider to be the A.W.E. mould?'

'Going by my one experience—middle-aged, loud voice, a bit sagging——' he made a double-handed gesture at his chest, '—and nice, neat, waved hair . . .' he eyed her expectantly.

'Well, thanks a lot.' She sniffed and put a hand to her nice, neat, curly hair then crossed her arms defensively over her generous bosom.

'—but no doubt, hearts of gold, Marlene,' Dave went on with a grin. 'What do we do about all the other ladies, Cort—while you're talking to their leader?'

'Hell, I don't know. That's your problem. Give them tea or coffee and smile a lot. The press will probably turn up and we mustn't forget our P.R. See if you can keep them out of my offices though, won't you, Dave? All except Milburn.'

'Will I get the security boys up here?'

'Good God no—we don't want to play the heavy. Just use that persuasive tongue of yours.'

Dave began to protest but Cort cut him short. 'Moral fibre, Dave. Moral fibre.' The younger man went out muttering something about batons and riot shields and Marlene was about to follow when Cort absently said:

'You can uncross your arms, Marlene. You don't suffer from middle-aged sag.'

She grinned. 'You noticed! All those exercises paid off.'

But Cort was studying the news report again.

'Blast!' he said under his breath.

'Are you going to be nice or nasty to Ms Milburn?' Marlene asked, feeling sorry for the woman in either case. At his most formidable Cort was a rock—pure granite. Tougher adversaries than a woman campaigner had tried to put the squeeze on Cort and failed. And when he decided to be charming—well, Marlene had often tried to evaluate in which mode he was more dangerous. There wasn't much in it.

'None of your business,' he said.

'Do her a favour and be nasty. It would be kinder, I think.'

The blue eyes glinted. 'I don't know why I put up with that kind of remark.'

'Yes you do. Because I'm a darned good secretary. And because I'm too old and too married to fall for all that tough attraction of yours.'

A few had in the past. There were, even now, several smitten female employees forever finding excuses to come up to the boardroom floor. If she hadn't been forty, four years older than Cort—and happily married—she could probably have fallen for him herself. As it was, she was fond of him and took liberties that a younger woman couldn't. She pointed out now and then, for instance, that none of his gorgeous girlfriends were a match for him. Cort had special qualities and he needed a special woman as she'd told him often. 'You find her for me, Marlene, and I'll consider her very carefully,' he always said.

'Get out of here,' he growled now. 'None of your sexy compliments so early in the day please. What would Charlie say?'

She laughed and went out. In the executive tearoom she set out cups, wondering how many cups of tea made up a demonstration. She returned to her desk with one ear tuned to the sound of the lift that might herald the arrival of A.W.E. and sympathised with earnest, sincere Abigail Milburn who was about to be 'cut out from the herd' and subjected to either Cort's toughness or his charm. She shook her head.

'Poor Abigail Milburn,' she muttered, 'This just isn't your day.'

An hour later, in the TITAN foyer Abigail Milburn looked over the restless crowd of women. Placards sprouted among the baby strollers and prams and handbags.

WINSTON—A VICTORY FOR BAD PLANNING said one, protesting with a Churchillian 'V' sign against the design of TITAN's Winston complex that would necessitate the removal of an avenue of sixty-year-old fig trees. Yesterday's on-site protest had only delayed the fate of the trees. Three had already been uprooted and the remaining nine were to be removed over the next week. There was little chance of saving them, Abby knew. TITAN had council permission to get rid of them in spite of progressive laws on selective site-clearing. But the issue had roused unexpected support from local residents and swelled into a resolution for further action after yesterday's violent but abortive attempt to get a stay of execution. So here they were.

TITAN—THE BIGGER THEY ARE, THE HARDER THEY FALL—another placard shouted. Abby smiled wryly at the optimism of it. They might have managed to stop work at Grady Hill while

historians and museum staff evaluated the church
remains, but TITAN would have its way eventually.
Giant companies like this invariably did. And groups
like theirs tore around like so many terriers, biting at
the giants' ankles and fighting to get publicity for their
cause. Wilderness was the headline-getting issue in
environment these days. People seemed less aware that
their cities were being turned into a new man-made
wilderness. A.W.E. was usually represented in the
press—when they were represented at all—as a bunch
of housewives fussing over a tree threatened by a
freeway, or an old cottage about to be demolished.

'The press is here, Abby,' Iris Broome said beside
her. 'And they seem to have worked out that you are
our leader. You can see why we chose you as
spokesperson, can't you?' she said drily as three men
pushed through the crowd towards Abby. 'With your
height and colouring you stand out like a sort of
antipodean Statue of Liberty.'

There was a sting in the words. Had she got the
votes, Iris would have enjoyed being spokesperson as
well as President of A.W.E.

'I'd like to think I can do more for A.W.E. than act
as a beacon,' Abby smiled. But she hadn't always been
able to smile about her extreme height. She was tall in
her stockinged feet and wearing the boots she had on
today was at least a half head above the other women.
Her cord jeans and sweater clung loyally to her
statuesque curves and accentuated the long line of her
legs, the narrow waist that flared to generous hips.
Her red hair was an unnecessary eye-catcher, Abby
had often thought, for one whose height already drew
enough attention. But she had long given up trying to
minimise it. Now it was thick and shoulder length,
cinched up into a fall at the back of her head. A
definite plus for a beacon.

The leading reporter looked her over and pursed his lips in a soundless whistle.

'*You're* Abigail Milburn?' he asked and eyed her wolfishly. With some difficulty Abby held on to her temper. She found it irritating that men had always to be persuaded to take her seriously. If she was a man he would be asking his first question by now. But because she was a female he was ogling her and possibly weighing up her potential as a bedmate. But—she reminded herself—he was Press. A magic word for A.W.E. Abby held out a hand to the man.

'Yes, I am. What paper are you from?'

He took her hand and told her, introducing himself as Joel Hamilton.

'I usually cover sports,' he said. 'But I'll take you rather than League any day.'

The rival press men were bored and not bothering to hide it. The only reason they were here at all, Abby knew, was that this was TITAN territory. They asked a few perfunctory questions and looked as if they might drift away until Hamilton asked her just what A.W.E. hoped to achieve today.

'We want to offer ourselves to TITAN—as a conscience,' she announced. At least it got their attention.

'Do you plan on speaking to the General Manager about your, er—offer?' Hamilton asked. 'Nicholsen?'

'No. To TITAN himself. Cort McKay. We're in A.W.E., Mr Hamilton, but not of chief executives.'

He gave a crack of laughter. 'Have you met him before, Miss Milburn?'

'I haven't had the pleasure,' she said, tongue in cheek.

'Great,' was all he said but with such relish that Abby knew a moment of unease. She shrugged it off, reflecting that if this man McKay turned out to be unpleasant it might make better news. He wouldn't, though. Cort McKay was one of the young Turks—and like others she had met, would be one of the breed. Paunch and public relations smile. Sympathy and understanding. 'I'm an environmentalist myself' one company director had told her soulfully, even as his factory pumped waste into a tiny creek. Of course by the time the government body involved took some action, he had tidied up his act and pleaded accidental leakage. Oh yes, she knew the type all right. In spite of his reputation as tough and direct, McKay would be a hypocrite on the issues they were fighting for. The elevators rose, carrying the ladies, the prams, the placards and the press to the seventeenth floor.

There was a young man waiting for them. Abby recognised him. He looked a bit nonplussed—perhaps he was trying to reconcile her appearance today with her bedraggled, raincoated one at the Grady Hill site.

'Hello, Mr Sinclair,' she said and he blinked, smiled and put out his arms as if to stop them. But Abby kept right on walking with the other women behind her and Dave Sinclair kept moving backwards, talking all the time. At the door of the executive suite, he made one last effort to turn them in another direction. Abby smiled.

'It's no use, Mr Sinclair. We've come to see Mr McKay himself. No one else will do.'

She swept past into the outer office, the others close behind. The woman at the desk snatched an arrangement of dried flowers to safety as A.W.E. packed in, knocking over a chair. A placard, showing TITAN as the serpent in the Garden of Eden—hardly an apt comparison when the garden was the city of Sydney—bumped a painting which clattered against the wall. A baby cried, voices swelled.

Just as Abby stepped towards the door marked C. A. McKay, it opened with an impatient whoosh.

'What the hell is going on?'

Cort McKay stood filling the doorway, his chin thrust forward and hands on hips. His eyes narrowed on Abby who hadn't stepped back but swivelled to face him, her own eyes not quite level with his. Her booted feet were apart, her hands on her hips in an unconscious copy of his stance. The baby was shushed by its mother. A few feet scuffed the floor, then near silence fell.

Cort McKay's eyes swept up and down, lingering on the generous curves of her figure, on the fall of russet hair that swayed behind her head. With great deliberation he did it all again. Abby's body tingled, her jaded nerve ends flared as he finished his inspection and held her sherry eyes with his own lightning-blue gaze.

'Abigail Milburn?' he said, with just a trace of amusement.

She made her own appraisal of the man while he looked her over. The tired old photograph of him that the press invariably used had not prepared her for the original. A desk man, his expense-account figure disguised in executive tailoring—that was what she'd expected. One of the breed. This man had no need of camouflage. His shoulders and chest tested the seams of his shirt, his pants outlined powerful thigh muscles and belted around a waist that was hard and flat-stomached. Abby had certainly not expected to confront a vital, muscular giant who looked as if he would be more at home tearing rocks apart with his bare hands. Titan himself, she thought—remembering her own prophetic phrase downstairs. But she was surprised, not intimidated.

'Mr McKay,' she said and put out her hand. Taking

the initiative with men like this often disconcerted them—offered her a small advantage. On this occasion she regretted it. McKay's hand swamped hers—his handshake was firm and warm and dry. There was enormous strength in his grasp. He didn't use it—but Abby felt it anyway. As the camera's flash took his attention from her to look around at the crowd and nod to the newspapermen, Abby promised herself caution.

'I'll talk to you alone,' he said, switching back to her suddenly. Without looking away again he said to Dave Sinclair,

'See that the ladies and the press get some coffee, will you, Dave?'

There was an ascending murmur from the crowd as Cort stood aside to allow Abby to enter his office and she was surprised that no one made an attempt to join her. Not even Iris who was plainly dissatisfied with the arrangement. Abby turned to him thoughtfully as he began to swing his door closed. A man of some personal power was Mr McKay. He paused for a moment—door just a few inches ajar—eyes narrowing on a glimpse of the serpent placard, wavering in the face of refreshment.

Then they were alone. The big chair creaked as Cort sat down. He rolled up a plan that was spread on the perspex desk, snapped a band around it. His large hands gathered up a few files and stacked them to one side near a water jug. Then he leaned back in the chair, arms folded across his chest, eyes on Abby. She was still standing, thinking that this was no figurehead's office but that of a man deeply involved with his business. A cabinet held wide drawers of blue-prints over by a window. He had a superb view of the harbour over the roofs of Milson's Point. A liner was just leaving Sydney's Overseas Terminal.

The tangle of farewell streamers was a cobweb from here.

'You seem to be paying us quite a bit of attention lately, Miss Milburn. It is Miss and not Mrs, I suppose?' He looked at her ringless left hand where it gripped the strap of her shoulder bag rather tighter than usual. Abby deliberately relaxed her hand. Why the sudden nerves, she asked herself?

'I hope you won't insist on Ms,' he went on. 'It sounds like the cry of a wounded mosquito.'

Smiling, she walked about the office, forcing him to follow her with his eyes. Psychologically it had to be better than sitting in the visitor's chair which was dwarfed by the massive desk and the man behind it.

'Yes, we have paid you some attention—yes, it is Miss not Mrs and yes, I agree—Ms sounds a lot like a wounded mosquito.'

His hard mouth pursed a little as if he might smile. But he didn't. Abby paused by a massive spotlit planter that spilled parlour palms and philodendron. She had a faint impression of defensiveness about the man. It must be wrong. He was big and impressive, formidable in both the personal and the corporate sense. According to the business magazines and her own private source Cort McKay was tough and resourceful and had fought his way to success through a maze of seemingly overwhelming odds. So— defensive? Not likely. Not faced with a woman representing a minority group that had no political teeth. Yet there was that guardedness in his eyes and those arms crossed over his chest in the traditional pose of self-protection . . . the fate of the Winston trees did not seem sufficient to account for it. In the last months since the Grady Hill episode she had read a lot about TITAN. Her private source had let slip that the company was planning a new kind of project—a resort

on a Barrier Reef island. Paradise, it was called and from
what Abby knew of it, the last thing an island called
Paradise needed was McKay's bulldozers. But the whole
area was under development and each island protected
by the National Parks government arm, so perhaps
TITAN would do no worse than any of the other
entrepreneurs in the tourist industry. It seemed mere
rumour though, for there was no talk of it in the papers
and business magazines. Unless TITAN was keeping it
under wraps for some reason. Still, that wouldn't be so
unusual. She walked over to the desk. It was the trees she
had to concentrate on. Nine trees planted as saplings
in memory of young men killed in the Great War, and
grown to old age instead of them.

'Come on, Miss Milburn, say what you want. I'm
busy.'

Careful, she warned herself again, and not just
against anger. Her quick instinct for caution surprised
her. Most things she took in her stride easily and here
she was already alerting her immune system.

'Your people were way out of line at Winston
yesterday, Mr McKay. They manhandled a number of
women who are prepared to lay charges.'

'They were obstructing work on private land.'

She couldn't deny that. It had been their object.
Work had been held up for hours while A.W.E.
members and residents had linked hands around the
fig trees.

'One of our supporters injured her knee. Several
had personal property destroyed.' Immune system?
Alerting her *immune* system? What on earth had made
her use a term like that, even in thought?

'Your supporters were the aggressors, Miss Milburn.
Maybe you should warn them of the dangers next
time.' His arms uncrossed—he looked almost com-
placent now, that odd wariness gone from him.

'TITAN's men removed two of our members—picked them up, six men to two women and took them on to the road none too gently.'

'Concern for their safety.'

'They'll be charged with assault.'

'You'll never make it stick.'

Abby looked over at the window, leaned a hand on his desk and sighed. 'No—I suppose we won't.'

In the silence she turned her head, met his gaze. He was frowning. She supposed he had a certain kind of attraction for those who liked that tough, macho image. He had a face that had been around all right.

'But I suppose we'll have to try——' she went on, '—make our statements, drag it through the papers— "Housewives claim compensation from building giants"—one of the T.V. current affairs programmes could be interested. It could go on for months, I suppose——'

'Am I supposed to feel threatened by that, Miss Milburn?' His voice had a grate to it. Like sand on the bottom of the bath after a day at the beach—like toast crumbs in bed. Her voice sharpened.

'You tell me, Mr McKay. Would harassment by a minority group threaten your nice, neat corporate image?'

The man was suddenly tense again. He crossed his arms.

'TITAN has broad shoulders.' he said.

Involuntarily her eyes dropped to his impressive shoulders.

'TITAN will need them if it continues to put up those acres of concrete it builds, Mr McKay. All those lovely Disneyland shopping complexes that are simply wonderful when they're opened and look grey and cheap a couple of years later . . .'

Instead of looking put out at her criticism he

actually seemed to like it. Abby was intrigued to see him relax, his hands resting easily along the arms of his chair.

'You're talking about a maintenance problem, not a building one.'

'Maintenance can't contend with a poor design—with concrete that cracks and tiles that fall off all too soon, colours that fade . . .'

It was the oddest feeling. Abby talked, said the words that always came feelingly—the words she'd said to other men like McKay. But this time her mind was separate. It was chalking up stupid little details. His thick, jet-black hair—the few threads of silver above his ears. An unusual combination—darkest hair, deep complexion, lightest blue eyes. Not everyone's idea of a typical Englishman. She concentrated on what she was saying . . . there was a harsh grain to the skin along his jaw although he was clean shaven—there was a bump on the bridge of his nose—her words came to a halt at last and she was free to put some control on the rovings of her mind.

He sat forward, pushed the jug of water towards her then picked up a tumbler and set it beside it. 'Your throat must be dry,' he said with a dryness of his own.

'If that's meant as a hint, Mr McKay, I'll ignore it. I came here to talk.' Pouring out some water, she raised her glass to him as if it was fine old wine. 'However, thank you for the drink.' Over the rim she saw his mouth curve. Saw too the speculative gleam in his eye. She put down the glass wondering what he would look like if he smiled, really smiled.

'I'm not your enemy, Miss Milburn. Only insofar as I am one of the public. That's where you should start your fight. With the consumers, with yourself. We build what *you* want. Tell yourself that you don't really need to drive everywhere and we can cut out the concrete carparks that offend you so. Shop at your corner store instead of dashing off to a multi-storied complex where you can pay on credit. You could put me out of business, Miss Milburn, if you could get people to alter their priorities. But let's not get into the realms of fantasy.'

Quite a speech, she thought, and gravely picked up the tumbler, polished its rim with her sleeve, then pushed both it and the water jug across the desk. She raised a brow in query and this time his smile was broad, displaying strong, white teeth. Abby blinked at the difference it made to his face. Not handsome. He would never be that. But with that smile he was ... dangerous.

'I'm not against the idea of shopping towns, Mr McKay, just the interpretation of the idea.'

'I just build. The men with the money decide what will be built.'

'Don't take me for a fool, Mr McKay,' Abby snapped. Dangerous? How could he be dangerous to her? 'We know that TITAN has invested heavily in some projects and retains managing interests in some. Namely the central coast condominiums. Of late you've become quite the entrepreneur. You aren't merely the instrument of others.'

Cort's eyes were alert again. What had she said to make that change in his expression?

'Done your homework, have you?' he clipped, his mouth set harshly.

'Yes, of course.' Her homework had yielded a few personal facts about the man too. His amazing success story and the vague details of a broken marriage left behind in England. His wife had run off with his friend, the story went, and taken their daughter with her. Looking at him, it was difficult to imagine him letting anything he wanted slip through his fingers.

'And what now, Miss Milburn?'

'Now?'

'Now that you've told me how all you ladies feel about things what's the next move?'

Her eyes narrowed. It was an odd question. Surely their next move was patently obvious. They had made all the fuss yesterday and today over the Winston trees, after all. She decided to play it by ear.

'I would say that *you* have something in mind.'

The dark eyebrows rose. 'Woman's intuition? I would have thought all traces of that had died of malnutrition in that independent, liberated soul of yours.'

She couldn't help it. Her mouth dropped open at his rudeness. Before she could frame a reply he went on, studying her heightened colour as he did so.

'Before you ladies take up arms again, I suggest that I talk to you. But I won't address a rag-tag protest group. I'm sure your committee would be pleased to snare a representative of evil commerce as guest speaker, so I'm prepared to appear at your next meeting to give TITAN's side of things and answer any questions.'

Interesting, Abby thought. A busy, powerful man like him—willing to address a minority group. The giant stooping to pet the terrier? Make friends with it? But why?

'Are you now?' she said softly and threw him a look that visibly disconcerted him. But he recovered quickly.

'Well, do you want me or not?' he snapped.

Abby opened her eyes wide. 'Would you care to re-phrase the question?'

He snorted and got up from his chair, leaving it shuddering with relief at the removal of his weight.

'It's a heroic offer, Mr McKay, and we'd love to

accept it, but regretfully can't agree to shelve our charges against your company meanwhile.'

'Then you're a fool.' Hands on hips, he shook his head. 'Your charges are trivial—TITAN's reputation won't be damaged by any of these laughable claims of assault.'

Her heart sank. She'd hoped that TITAN might prefer to accede to their demands about the trees, rather than risk the unattractive publicity of legal action, but it wasn't going to work. She thought of those nine remaining figs and gave it a last shot.

'If TITAN puts its carpark costings before the will of the residents near Winston, A.W.E. will just have to assume it is totally irresponsible. Which means that we might have to start looking into *all* your projects, Mr McKay——' It was feeble and she knew it. The terrier threatening to yap at the heels of the giant unless he gave in. It might be inconvenient for TITAN but no more than that. She waited for McKay to laugh in her face. He didn't. In fact the venomous quality of his silence almost sent her running. Cort McKay gave her a hard, blazing look.

'You've brought work to a standstill at Grady Hill and lost us hours at Winston. What exactly are you after, Miss Milburn?'

'The trees of course.' Wasn't that obvious? What else did he think they were after? 'I'm sure you'll find a way to concrete over the church foundations eventually but we would like you to use a little TITAN ingenuity to landscape around that avenue of figs. They've been sixty years in the growing—and in their way a memorial to the young men of the district killed in war. Surely there is room for them on the site where those young men's families and descendants might do their shopping.' She paused, added drily,

'You could use that as part of your promotion—the human interest touch.'

He stared unblinkingly at her.

'Very well, Miss Milburn,' he said at last. 'You've convinced me. The trees will stay. I'll phone through new instructions now if you agree to drop your ridiculous charges.'

Hiding her elation and her staggering surprise, Abby nodded.

Cort McKay was too shrewd not to know that everything she'd said was dramatised, inflated—one big bluff. A man like him would deal summarily with what he had himself called 'laughable claims'. Yet he had conceded—so quickly. He gave his orders over the phone and looked up to catch her watching him. There was some small reaction at her expression but just what it was she couldn't be sure.

'Congratulations,' he put the phone down, kept his hand on it a moment. Bit, capable hands he had. 'You've won.'

CHAPTER TWO

CIRCLING the desk he came and stood near her and Abby became uncomfortably aware of his size and strength. The rolled up sleeves of his blue shirt exposed the powerful shape of his arms and as he put hands to his hips, the fabric pulled across the powerhouse chest. It was a rare thing for her to feel crowded by anyone.

'What do you do for a living, Miss Milburn? Who do you work for?' He was relaxed now. Totally relaxed. Abby felt her own muscles tighten.

'Nobody. I run my own business.'

'What kind?'

'Is that relevant?'

'You know what I do,' he pointed out as if it was only fair she even the score. Abby stared at him a moment.

'A music store. I sell instruments, music, teachers' supplies.'

He laughed. 'What do you do? Stand over them and intimidate them into buying?'

'Jokes about height have no sting coming from *you*, Mr McKay.' Again the laugh. Did he imagine that reminding her she was too tall for femininity would put her at a disadvantage?

'What do you call your music store?'

'Monster Music,' she snapped, annoyed at herself for caring after all. 'Abby's Music actually. Though what all this has to do with our dealings I can't see.'

'Can't you?' His eyes held hers and she felt an unusual flash of fear. Quite abruptly all those separate attributes she had noticed were combined into a dangerous, dynamic whole. A pause while he eyed her figure again. 'You're a tall girl to be wearing heels that high. Most women your height would wear low heels so that they didn't loom over their menfolk.'

'I never consider my menfolk when I buy my shoes—only myself. That's another womanly instinct that must have died of malnutrition.'

'That was rude of me.'

'Yes, it was.'

'True, but rude.' He watched her closely, noticing the faint tinge of colour high on her cheeks.

'Even your apologies are insulting, Mr McKay. Does my independence affront your views on what a woman should be?'

'No. It doesn't affront me. But it makes me wonder what you're hiding behind it.'

She had the feeling that he could see further than she wanted. Abby quelled the urge to run from him. It had been hard work building her armour and if there were still a few chinks in it, she didn't want this man to discover them.

'You really are obnoxious.'

'Abby's Music——' he murmured, unperturbed. 'So I assume your friends call you Abby. May I?'

She stared. 'No. You may not. You're not a friend and this discussion is over.'

'As the winner in this confrontation you can afford to be gracious, Abby——' He was *so* relaxed. Somehow she didn't think he would usually be so philosophical about giving way to pressure even over a fairly insignificant issue for TITAN.

'I don't know why it is, Mr McKay—but I feel as if we've been fobbed off with a—a consolation prize.'

He looked down for a moment. What incredible, thick, black lashes the man had. A touch of luxury in a

Spartan setting. The impact of his extraordinarily light, extraordinarily blue eyes was all the more potent when he looked up again.

'Have dinner with me tonight,' he said softly. Not a question really.

'Why?'

'I get hungry,' he explained, 'Don't you?'

Her lips twitched. 'Yes. But no thanks.'

There was something worrying about this change of pace. Abby couldn't pin it down. And she was not entirely unattracted by the idea of sitting opposite this man over dinner, finding out what went on inside that rugged head of his.

'You're—tied up?' he pressed.

'No.'

'I'm not married,' he assured her, as if that might be the obstacle.

'How interesting.'

'You don't like me,' he said with a sad spaniel look. Or as close as he could manage with his arrogant, super-masculine looks. Why was he turning on the charm?

'I'm sure that will worry you sick,' she said and he grinned. Oh boy, she thought—a smile like that could burn holes in the strongest resolution. 'Shall we go and tell the press all about it, Mr McKay?' she added briskly.

'You think they'll be interested that I asked you to dinner?'

'Don't be facetious.'

'It's an improvement on obnoxious.' He walked alongside her, leaned across to take the door handle. Abby stopped, unwilling to remain there just inches from him and equally unwilling to back off.

'Did you carry a placard, Abby?'

She shook her head.

'Ah. I thought you might have been wielding that monstrosity with the snake on it.'

'TITAN as the serpent in paradise?' she said with gentle malice and so close, saw the change in his eyes. So fleeting she might have imagined it at longer range. What had she said? TITAN as the serpent . . . in paradise . . . Paradise? The island. Was *that* what had made Mr McKay so wary? 'We might have to start looking into *all* your projects——' He'd looked like thunder at that. Perhaps the island resort wasn't a rumour then. Which meant that TITAN was keeping it quiet. It would be interesting to know why if a man like McKay let himself be thrown by it.

'Are you going to open the door, Mr McKay, or will I need to call for help?'

'Not this time.'

'That sounds ominous—almost like a threat.'

'I never need to use threats,' and though he smiled, Abby could believe it. 'I just don't let anyone get in my way—not unless I want them to.'

A warning? And if so, what kind? Cort leaned closer as he turned the door handle. A drift of some after-shave or soap reached her and a stab of sensation as if she had touched an exposed electric wire. She went into the outer office with an odd shifting feeling inside her.

'A.W.E. came here to offer themselves to you as a conscience. Will you take them up on it?' Joel Hamilton asked the TITAN boss, tongue in cheek.

'Some offers are hard to refuse,' the big man said and looked directly at Abby with a sexy smile. 'Abby—I mean Miss Milburn can be very—persuasive.' He made it sound as if she'd lured him on to a couch. Abby fulminated. 'In fact, she talked me into preserving the trees on the Winston site.'

A cheer broke out from the women and Cort

McKay actually had the gall to give a slight bow. He made some flowery statements about the great age of the trees, the inadvertent short-sightedness of TITAN in not recognising their value and gave full marks to A.W.E. for alerting him to it, while managing to retain the credit for himself. Abby came in with some fairly flowery stuff herself, managing to correct a few, not all, of his clever hints about the nature of their interview. She finished up by informing the reporters that the TITAN boss had simply *insisted* on attending their next meeting—as a representative of evil commerce. Hamilton wrote it down, got the time and the place which rather committed Mr McKay. His original offer she knew had been a diversion. He hardly would want to address their meeting now that he had capitulated on the trees. Lips twitching Abby watched him control his annoyance.

'Was that my suggestion, Abby?' His use of her first name jarred. He made it sound amazingly intimate, did a great impersonation of a man bowled over. He ogled her legs. Boldly eyed her figure. From spokesperson on serious matters to sex object in a matter of minutes, Abby fumed.

'Yes, it was your idea. And I hope you'll remember how eager you were to come when we get you in the hot seat. We have several questions to put to you that might have you wishing you were marooned on a desert island.'

That chilled a little of his false ardour. Though he smiled, he was wary again at her phrasing.

Joel Hamilton asked a few more questions and everyone gradually filed out. As the last stragglers went Cort called her back.

'Abby——'

She walked back a pace or two. Dave Sinclair stood behind his boss, an odd mix of curiosity and anxiety on his thin face. The secretary was openly fascinated. Abby could only suppose she didn't see people stand up to her boss very often.

'—you know very well I didn't expect to honour that offer of mine once you had what you wanted.'

'Tough. I didn't expect to have our business meeting represented to the press as some kind of personal interlude. So it serves you right that you'll have to take the hot seat at our next meeting—try to make a romance out of that!'

Cort stuck his hands on his hips. 'Be careful Abby.'

She aped his stance. 'Why, Mr McKay—I'm just *shaking* in my boots.'

With a flick of her thick, russet hair she was gone.

Cort looked at his offsider.

'A "great, big, hulking woman",' he quoted. 'Better get your eyes tested, Dave.'

'What do you think, Marlene, old girl?' Dave Sinclair asked after Cort had slammed shut his office door.

'I hate to have to admit it, but I think the boss has met his match.'

She went to her desk, began punching in some data on her computer. After Dave too had gone, Marlene looked at Cort's door and nested her chin on her hand. She wondered what the boss would say if she told him that she might—at last—have found a woman for him to consider. Very carefully.

Their wishes for publicity had been granted with a vengeance, Abby thought the next day. But as in all the old morality tales, wishes granted held a catch.

TITAN AND THE AMAZON Joel Hamilton had headed his article. Thankfully a politician had crossed the floor to vote with the opposition and the front and second pages were full. The photograph of

Cort McKay and Abby Milburn confronting each
other at his office door appeared on the third page.

'—Tough boss of TITAN, Cort McKay might have
met his match in the dynamic Abigail Milburn, not
only an articulate spokesperson for A.W.E. but a
beautiful, intelligent woman. Miss Milburn talked Mr
McKay into saving the sixty-year-old trees due for
removal from the company's Winston Shoppingtown
site. 'She is very persuasive,' Mr McKay said of the
tall, striking redhead. Miss Milburn offered herself
and fellow A.W.E. members to TITAN as a
conscience. 'Some offers are hard to refuse,' Mr
McKay admitted after a private discussion with Miss
Milburn——'

Joel Hamilton certainly seemed to be making the
most of his secondment from the sports pages.

There was more—the most pleasing bits being those
that committed Cort McKay to addressing their next
meeting. The big man wouldn't like that. He could
hardly back down when the newspaper might decide
to cover the event. There was no doubt that A.W.E.
came off rather better in this article than previously
but there was a little too much of Abby Milburn in it
for her liking. The whole thing sounded like a clash of
personalities—hers and McKay's, leavened with strong
hints of a love/hate relationship that made her grit her
teeth. A.W.E. wasn't going to like that.

It was a reasonable photograph of her. In profile she
fitted Joel Hamilton's exaggerated claims of beautiful,
striking. In fact her mouth was a fraction too wide, her
nose ordinary and faintly freckled and her eyes too
wide-spaced. But side on her bone structure featured
and that was, Abby knew, the strength of her face.
Cort McKay did not fare so well in profile. The
camera hadn't captured more than the physical
irregularities that in reality were oddly attractive.

Rising, she flung the paper down on to the breakfast
table.

'Titan and the Amazon!' Joel Hamilton should stick
to covering sports. But when she made coffee and sat
down, her eyes returned again and again to the face of
McKay. He was tough all right as the article stated and
their victory had been too easily wrested from such a
man. People like him only gave away points when it
was in their interests. The Paradise resort . . . she
thought, and wondered. But perhaps she should forget
about his possible secrets. After all, if there was
anything about the island to interest A.W.E. it would
become known sooner or later.

'Have dinner with me tonight——' What if she had
said yes? It might have been interesting . . . Abby felt
that shifting sensation again. The man was shrewd and
ruthless. But there was something about him—that
smile, the dry sense of humour and, she admitted with
reluctance, a certain sex appeal that made her feel as if
her back was to the wall. Yes. Definitely she would
leave the matter of Paradise alone. For the moment.

'Congratulations,' Iris Broome said stiffly to her on
the phone at Abby's Music later that morning. 'You're
a star.' As if Abby had arranged the entire
demonstration for that purpose.

'Iris, I don't care for the style of Hamilton's article
either. But I can't change that. We got what we
wanted and publicity into the bargain.'

Iris couldn't refute that and rang off in fairly
friendly fashion, but Abby guessed that neither she
nor other members would be so warm to her in future
in spite of her success. By singling her out and
labelling her 'a beautiful, intelligent woman' Hamilton
had given her a status separate from the group.

The Crows Nest traffic hummed on the Pacific
Highway as she sat in her tiny office, updating her

books and formulating advance Christmas orders. The task was less absorbing than she would have liked. With a sigh, she put her paperwork away and tidied her desk, then walked through to the adjoining room which she laughingly called her studio. Several guitars stood there and she picked one up and swiftly tuned it, playing a snatch of a pop song that she taught her students. Nowadays her teaching was the only playing she did, apart from the occasional session at home. Finding time to play purely for pleasure was becoming steadily more difficult even though she off-loaded her advanced students on to an eager young man who needed the money. Paul Donaldson came in two nights a week and taught several students here in the studio while she did the same in the shop downstairs.

Putting the guitar down, she smiled. If the business could afford it, she could easily talk Paul into teaching every night. At twenty-four he was the father of three with a fourth child on the way and a need to augment his clerical wage to support his brood.

'I hope you've been rushed off your feet,' she said to her assistant when she went downstairs to the shop.

'Oh no,' Helen assured her earnestly, 'it's been very quiet.'

'I was kidding.' Abby wished that Helen had a sense of humour. But she was such a willing, pleasant woman that it seemed churlish to want humour too. With an absolutely straight face she checked the big, glass display case under the counter and saw that the items had been changed around again. She could feel Helen's eyes on her as she put everything back the way it was. It was a non-verbalised game between them. Abby arranged the shop window and the displays inside and Helen used a variety of excuses in order to change them. 'I was just dusting,' she'd say to explain the guitar moved a foot to the right, the cornet gleaming further up the wall. To Abby it was a source of constant amusement and she only put everything back to see if Helen would ever come out in the open and defend her own arrangement. But she never did.

'What did Mr Salford say about your photo in the paper today?' Helen wanted to know, her mouse-brown eyes big with curiosity.

'I haven't spoken to Martin. Anyway what should he say?'

'Oh, I just thought he mightn't like seeing you and that TITAN man looking so . . .' she hesitated when Abby looked sharply at her. 'Him being your boyfriend . . .'

'Looking so—what?'

'Well—absorbed, I suppose.'

Absorbed. Abby rubbed a cloth over the glass counter top. It wasn't just the recognition of a powerful opponent that had locked her eyes with McKay's—there had been something else . . .

'We were both in profile, Helen. And you know what they say. You can't tell what's going on in someone's head from a profile.' Her tone was light, voice bouncing a bit as she rubbed the glass vigorously.

'Do they?'

'Do they what?'

'Say that about profiles?'

Oh lord, Abby thought and gravely assured Helen that 'they' did.

'What is he like?'

'Cort McKay?' Abby firmed her lips. 'He's a cunning, ruthless man who'll do just about anything to get what he wants.'

Helen's eyes rounded. 'I didn't think people like that really existed,' she said. 'He sounds like someone out of a film. Or a television serial.'

Abby laughed out loud at that. Her assistant's life

revolved around her quiet accountant husband, her two children and several soap operas. Her perfectly serious comparison of the tough, realistic McKay with one of her cardboard villains was ludicrous.

'Helen, no. McKay's too much man for one of your serials.' As soon as she said it she could have bitten her tongue. Helen's eyes were positively alight at that 'too much man'.

'Oh,' she said with rounded mouth and eyes, and took it quite the wrong way. Her eyes grew rounder still that afternoon when Abby opened a small parcel delivered by courier. It contained perfume in an extravagant box.

'Isn't that the perfume you always wear? Who sent it? Oh, I suppose it was Mr Salford.' Helen's nose was almost quivering with inquisitiveness.

'No—it isn't from Martin——' The courier was waiting for a reply, he said—Martin didn't do things in this grand manner. Even before she opened the note Abby had that odd feeling of insecurity. As if something solid shifted beneath her feet.

'Have dinner with me tonight,' it said. 'Cort.'

She stared at the perfume and knew it was no coincidence that he'd sent her favourite. That was the disturbing thing about it. He'd noticed she was wearing it yesterday, identified it. So what else had he noticed? Abby folded the note and stuck it in her skirt pocket, wondering why she got a sudden image of Cort McKay in hunter's gear, looking down rifle sights at her.

'Is it from—him?' Helen asked, imbuing the pronoun with a sort of awe.

'Yes. But I'll send it back.' She re-wrapped it, including one of her business cards with 'no' written on the back. The courier took it away; Helen speculated on why the TITAN boss had sent perfume to the A.W.E. spokesperson but gave up when she got no encouragement from Abby.

It was eight o'clock that evening before Abby finished with her last student and another half hour before Paul Donaldson ushered his out.

'Whew,' he shook his head, 'I can use a break from Scarborough Fair.'

'Count your blessings that I take the beginners,' Abby retorted. 'Camptown Races and Yankee Doodle.'

They laughed, but over their usual cup of coffee, Paul gave her an anxious look.

'Um—Abby—this business about A.W.E. and TITAN——'

She knew what he would say. He needed the extra dollars he picked up by teaching her students, as well as his job at TITAN and her lobbying against his major employer was making him nervous.

'Anything I might have sort of, confided about TITAN—I hope you wouldn't use it. If Mr McKay found out he might think I was spying for you.'

He laughed at the idea, but nervously. All the press exposure over Grady Hill and now Winston was bound to bother him. She was in fact a little guilty that it was Paul's careless talk and her own subsequent promptings that had first made her think the company had something planned for Paradise. But Paul would never be looked upon as an informant even if TITAN ever had reason to look for one. He was merely a clerk in the accounts department and it was his membership of the staff squash club that had allowed him to overhear talk about the resort. It was all academic— she had already decided not to confide her suspicions about Paradise to the A.W.E. Committee.

'You haven't told me anything we didn't already know,' she lied to put his mind at rest. But how to put her own mind at rest? In her pocket, her fingers touched the tiny folded note that had accompanied the perfume. Cort McKay in hunter's gear, she thought uneasily . . . On impulse she added, 'TITAN must be almost due to commence building the crew accommodation by now.'

'Next month from what I hear. The helicopter service is operating from the mainland——' Paul caught back the words in embarrassment and Abby hid her satisfaction. It was worth a little guilt to have some ammunition against Mr McKay. His note rustled between her fingers. Abby didn't question why she should suddenly ditch her earlier resolution to let the matter lie. Or why she should need ammunition.

'Don't worry about it, Paul. As I said, we knew about it anyway. Now—can you manage another half-hour on Wednesdays—there's a new advanced student . . .'

It was around nine-fifteen when she got home and the phone was ringing. She opened the door and dashed to answer it.

'Yes?' she said breathlessly.

'Hello, Abby. You sound out of breath. I hope I'm not disturbing you?'

Oh, but he was. Abby didn't even bother going through the ritual of asking who it was. It was Cort McKay and he knew that she knew. No point in wasting time on coyness where he was concerned.

'What do you want, Mr McKay?'

'I got your answer. But why send my perfume back? Did I get it wrong? That *was* Guerlain you were wearing yesterday, wasn't it?—I had to test several bottles to identify it.' She had a mental picture of him looming at a perfume counter, sniffing tiny little French scent bottles until he got the right one. It had a certain humour to it.

'You got it right—and you got it wrong. I want no gifts from you, not even my favourite perfume.'

'Have dinner with me then—tomorrow night——'

'No.'

'A drink——?'

'No.'

'You might like to hear my plans for Grady Hill.'

'Why would I want to hear those? You'll no doubt pave right over the old church site.'

'Of course I won't. It's history. I might be a Pom but some of my ancestors came out here in the old days—assisted passage you might say. There's an Aussie branch of my family somewhere if I took the trouble to trace it.'

'Look for large areas of concrete,' she suggested. 'Good night, Mr McKay.'

It unsettled her, sent her about her apartment unnecessarily moving books, neatening shelves. He made her feel so threatened. Why was that? She knew the answer and let it lie waiting at the back of her mind.

In the morning it would wait no more. For beside the milk and newspaper outside her door was the Guerlain perfume. Abby clutched her robe to her as if McKay himself might be somewhere around. Had he brought it here? And if so, when? She picked everything up quickly and slammed the door, stood there looking at it with a cornered feeling. Had he brought it last night while she tossed in her bed—or just minutes ago?

The perfume sat on the table, incongruous next to the marmalade and Abby admitted why Cort McKay bothered her. He was crowding her—pursuing. It was pretty obvious that his reasons were connected with A.W.E. He wanted to know perhaps whether she had any concrete knowledge of the Paradise resort. But whatever his reasons, Abby recognised her danger. Only one other man had got close enough to use his wits and charm against her. Since Simon she'd not allowed anyone that close. But Cort McKay might not wait to be allowed.

She gave a small, dry laugh, eyes fixed on the perfume but faraway. The two men might share a determination to have their own way, but there any comparison ended. The big man with his rugged face was nothing like Simon Castle. A golden boy, that was Simon. Twenty-five when she'd met him, he was blonde, handsome, trendy. He was studying law and living in the fine style provided by his parents. He had loads of boyish appeal and perfect manners which endeared him to the older generation. Her parents were delighted with him. They had actually looked with hope upon the disappointing daughter who failed to follow their son into academic glory. Professors both, with physics and mathematics soundly covered between them and academic success their yardstick, they had shown a certain warmth to Abby when she began seeing Simon. He was 'just the kind of young man we hoped to see you with' and 'a boy with a bright future'. Of course a scientist would have been better, but a promising law student drew her parents' approval. Abby felt a glow of pleasure at the time. She couldn't remember ever winning such approval before. When her brother Zach had taken up a scholarship in the States, Abby thought she might receive the overflow of attention reserved for him. But not until Simon came long did she warrant that.

Unsure of herself, disliking her extreme height and her awkward colouring, Abby was the opposite of the confident Simon. When he sought her out she was amazed, grateful. He became the recipient of all the frustrated love and affection that her cool, preoccupied parents never seemed to want from her. And he gained for her the approval she'd always craved. She was in love with him within a month. Later she saw all too clearly that she had been easy prey. Her longing to belong somewhere, to someone, had blinded her to Simon's less attractive side. The clean-cut image hid the spoilt, pampered boy he was. His manners masked a selfish determination to get what he wanted. And he wanted Abby.

What Simon wanted—he got. Eventually, one night when he was a little less than sober, he shed his beautiful manners and took it. For a few minutes she was bewildered, panicked by his forcefulness, but her sudden, spirited resistance melted before the one ultimate persuasion.

'Come on Abby—I love you,' he said. 'Love me.'

They were the magic words, the ones she had been waiting for and Abby pushed aside her doubts and fears for the man she loved. The words were to be the only magic of the experience she had dreamed about. But she was crazy for Simon, swept into their affair on his careless talk of an engagement ring—one day—and a lifetime together—as soon as he was established in his career. But the lifetime together became a subject Simon avoided and somehow Abby never found the magic she expected with him. Simon was furious when she mentioned it. He gave her a sound reason for it. She was cold, he said. Some women were like that, he said. Unable to find pleasure in physical love. Frigid. He'd applied the word to her without hesitation and found himself a new girlfriend.

Her parents were upset to lose the son-in-law Simon had had no intention of ever being. And with him went the approval they had finally given her. That was when she had begun to build her armour.

The Guerlain package mocked her. In six years she

still hadn't stoppered up some of the cracks. 'Your independence doesn't bother me but it makes me wonder what you're hiding behind it——' Cort McKay had said and she'd felt like running. Now a knot tightened in her stomach and Abby felt the old flutter of fear. Hesitant, shy, dependent Abigail had become outspoken, fiercely independent Abby. It had taken years but she had forced herself to face the things she feared. The shop was a success. Her fears all outfaced. Except one. In six years she could not bring herself to repeat her experiences with Simon, even though with maturity she realised that he had been supremely selfish lover. Now she admitted to herself that the very thing of which she was scared, was probably true. She could well be frigid—a terrifying thing to be in this age of sexual freedom and fulfilment. But at twenty-six Abby was everything else she had aimed to be. She had come to grips with her unusual looks, the red hair that she had once hated, the height for which she had once apologised. A beautiful and intelligent woman, the reporter had described her. Abby gave a wry smile. She'd come a long way. But the scars were there. And somehow, Cort McKay knew.

She finished her breakfast and cleared the table until only the elegant French package stood there. It was still there when she left to open the shop. And although she worked and smiled and accepted a half-dozen calls of congratulations over the Winston trees episode, Cort McKay's perfume and his motives were still on her mind when the phone rang yet again just before closing time. Helen had gone and Abby went behind the half screen that shielded the phone from the door.

It was a call she'd been expecting but even so, she stiffened at her mother's cool, precise voice. It was even more precise than usual which meant that she was outraged. How *could* a daughter of hers be photographed like that—standing there trading stares with that man in that intimate way? Intimate? Abby swallowed. Those odd vibrations between her and Cort McKay had reached through the blandness of newsprint, even to her mother it seemed.

'Your father was embarrassed to admit you were his daughter.' Which meant she had been too. That was the crux of the matter. The two professors Milburn were happy to claim parental credit for Zach—but a daughter, degree-less, single and harrying the establishment from time to time, could not add lustre to the family name.

'What's new, Mother? He's been embarrassed to admit I was his daughter for years. So have you.'

There was a brief silence. Abby pictured her mother running a thin, clever hand over her chignon.

'Now don't snap at me, Abigail. You can't expect us to like this brashness of yours. We don't care to see you making a fool of yourself. Titan and the Amazon!' she clicked her tongue in distaste. 'It's so incredibly vulgar.'

'There are worse labels than Amazon, Mother.'

'Well, do try to stay out of that kind of thing. It's time you settled down with a husband and started a family. You're twenty-seven now and if you want children you should be thinking about it soon. Your father and I would rather like grandchildren.'

Abby gave a snort of laughter to hide her hurt and resisted the impulse to suggest they talk Zach into procreating.

'I'm twenty-*six* Mother, and unlikely to ever present you with grandchildren.'

Her mother ignored that and in a transparent change of subject began to relate the contents of a rare letter from Zach who lived permanently in the States now.

'—he may be flying over for a visit though he doesn't state when exactly——' Zach had turned down a job offer from NASA. Zach could have taken his pick of funding for his research. But Zach had opened his own commercial laboratory. Abby couldn't be sure but there was a hint of disapproval on this last—only a hint. For whatever turn his career took, Zach was not featuring as a laughing stock in the papers. The adulation of her older brother had begun early and though it had made Zach a little more arrogant, a little more superior than average, it had affected Abby more as she hung about on the outside—looking in.

'Yes Mother—wonderful—great.' As always the call was terminated with a vague, dutiful invitation to dinner. Dinner and lectures, Abby thought wryly.

'But phone first, Abigail—your father and I have a full schedule.'

Abby put the phone down. Their schedule always had been full. Not too full to attend speech nights and graduations for Zach where he carried off barrows full of trophies and certificates, but usually too occupied to see Abby receive her occasional bouquet. There was a hint of the old wistfulness in her sherry-gold eyes as she rounded the screen to lock the shop doors. She pulled up sharply at the sight of the man inspecting the contents of the display counter.

CHAPTER THREE

CORT turned his head. He flicked a glance over her slim fitting pants and the matching rust shirt that skimmed the contours of her breasts and tucked into her waist. His eyes came back to her face and her hair that waved loose to her shoulders.

Abby was aware of the slam of her pulse. She checked a need to adjust her shirt, touch her hair. Why on earth did this man make holding on to her confidence a conscious thing?

'What do you want?'

'Do you greet all your customers with such warmth?'

'You're not a customer.'

'Of course I'm a customer,' he grinned. 'What other reason could I have for calling on you at your business address?' He leaned back against the counter, one leg crossed over the other, his big hands resting lightly on his hips hooking back the edges of the fine wool jacket he wore. His chest muscles strained against the top two buttons of his open-necked business shirt, pulling the fabric sideways. Through the keyhole Abby could see dark curling chest hair. She raised her eyes suddenly and surprised a peculiar expression on his face.

'That, Mr McKay, is what I'd like to know.'

Straightening, he took a step forward which brought him within inches of her. Her instinctive jerk away was firmly controlled but a fraction too late. There was a gleam in his eyes that told her he'd seen it.

'I have no ulterior motive, Abby.'

44

Liar, her senses screamed as she forced herself to remain there, close enough to see the lines about his eyes, the fine silver threads in his dark hair. The tough-hewn jaw had just a hint of shadow to it. It would be rough to the touch ... Abby turned away sharply.

'Did you send someone to my place with that perfume or were you lurking about in person, Mr McKay?'

'Lurking?' he echoed and held both arms out wide to invite her inspection. 'I'm not built for lurking, Abby.'

She had a swift vision of Cort McKay trying to hide himself behind a lamp-post. The humour of it touched a smile to her mouth and she had to force back her laughter.

'I was passing and returned the perfume this morning. Of course I ran the risk that you might merely think the milkman was romancing you.'

She smiled again. 'For a man in your position you really are ridiculous.'

'Hmmm—from obnoxious to facetious to ridiculous. Is it a promising trend, do you think?'

Trend. She didn't like the sound of that. 'How did you know where I lived?'

'The phone book. I phoned two other A. Milburns before I reached you last night.'

Abby's heart pounded. Cort McKay, working his way through the phone book to get in touch with her? She felt crowded again.

'Mr McKay, I'm just about to close up shop so will you come to the point of your visit?'

'By all means,' he said and advanced on her until she stepped back and bumped the wall. His arms reached out either side of her and Abby froze as that tough face came close to hers. A mild shock buzzed to every part of her as his body touched hers, then he was stretching over her head and the soft cloth of his shirt touched her chin.

A bass note twanged, resounded as he lifted a guitar from the overhead wall display.

'I want to buy a guitar. This one looks good.' Stonily she told him that it should look good and the price that guaranteed it, and stayed there, her back to the wall. His hands were gentle, almost caressing on the smooth, polished wood of the long neck. He turned the instrument over, ran his fingertips lightly over the voluptuous curves of the guitar's body. Such large hands with long, squared-off fingers but they moved over the guitar's surface lovingly. One palm cupped the rounded back of the neck and moved slowly up, then down—his thumb brushed the edges of the brass frets. So much strength channelled into tenderness . . . Abby looked up and found that he was not watching the guitar as she had thought. He was watching her. She was startled that she had almost been able to feel his hands on her, so evocative were they—and was horrified that he might know it.

'Tune it for me.' He regarded the flush on her skin as he handed her the guitar. Abby avoided his hands in the exchange. There was intimacy enough in touching the mellow wood which he had caressed. Putting her foot on a rest, she bent her head and adjusted the tuning keys. Her hair fell forward and hid the man and his odd expression. The strings responded to her touch and she rippled off a few bars of Greensleeves in a delicate finger-picking pattern. The familiar motions restored her confidence— reminded her of how far she'd come these last six years. Aimlessly she strummed a few chords to let her assurance build, then on impulse broke into the opening bars of 'Stranger in Paradise'. It was good, so good to look up at him and see the cool edge of caution in those confident eyes. She had after all, some ammunition against Cort McKay.

'Well, Mr McKay, what do you think?'

'I'll take it.'

'What, no comparisons? Maybe I have something else that you'd like better?'

'Maybe you do.' A long, admiring look and the devil in those light-blue eyes.

'Guitars I mean.'

'But what else?' he mocked.

'Are you really going to buy it?'

'You'll end up out of business if you treat your customers like this. When I say I want something, Abby—I mean it.'

Sharply she looked up at the double-edged words and was irritated by the slam of her heart beat.

'Can you play the guitar?' she asked sceptically. He turned a mock-wounded look on her that forced a smile to her lips.

'Of course. I'm not just a pretty face you know.'

Her laughter was clear and full and surprised her as much as it did Cort. Abby turned quickly from the arrested expression on his craggy, far from pretty face.

'All right, Mr McKay—I'll take you at face value. Thank you for your custom.'

Behind the screen she put the money in her cash bag and wrote out a docket.

'Here's your receipt,' she began but stopped as she came to the counter and saw him turning over the CLOSED sign and shooting the upper and lower bolts of the shop's front door.

'You did say you were closing—and I want to talk to you uninterrupted,' he explained as she tried to disguise her uneasiness.

'You said no ulterior motives, Mr McKay.'

His grin was disarming. 'Just trying to put you at ease, Abby. You seemed—nervous of me. But I did genuinely want a guitar.'

'Mr McKay, I'm tired and I want to go home. You've got a nerve to come here wanting discussions at a time that just happens to suit you.'

'You came to my office first.'

Abby considered. This was no place to be closeted with him—in her shop with night falling. Yet it was a chance to find out what it was about the island that was bugging him enough to send him in pursuit with his perfume and phone calls. And now, house calls.

'Very well.' Deep down she knew she shouldn't be saying this. Her advantage was small, too small to gamble with. But some rebellious part of her wanted to wipe out that stupid blushing weakness of hers earlier. 'Come upstairs and talk. I can offer you some coffee.'

'Do you know I expected you to put up a fight?'

Dispassionately she regarded his big frame. 'Would it do any good? I might be an Amazon but I'm hardly able to throw you out, am I?'

The sound of his laughter was deep and rich. Abby liked the rumble of it here in the tiny, darkening shop.

'That might be difficult even for you,' he said, amused.

As she started up the stairs, Abby wondered if he had ever been physically bested. With that build it was dubious that anyone would have the nerve to contemplate force with him. He was a few steps behind her, his weight sending a tremor through the open treads.

'My office is on a somewhat smaller scale than your own,' she warned him, 'And you'll get no fancy views.'

'On the contrary,' he murmured and she looked

over her shoulder to see his eyes fixed on her behind, 'the views are among the best I've seen.'

In spite of herself she smiled at his mock innocent face.

'You're an expert I suppose – on views.'

'I've seen a few,' he admitted modestly as they walked into the office. Abby switched on the light and he wandered around the adjoining studio while she made coffee at a jug-sized counter and a fist-sized sink. The walls were covered with posters—Yamaha advertisements, and Gibson. Kevin Borich, George Benson, Chuck Mangione and James Galway. There were also two music theory charts.

'Do you teach guitar?' he asked as she put the coffee on the desk.

'Yes. Beginners mostly.'

'That must have its difficulties.'

'Not at all—I simply stand over them and intimidate them into playing.'

'You remember that? Did my rather corny joke sting?'

'I'm five foot eleven, Mr McKay, and used to corny jokes about my height. Now,' she sat back in her chair and looked at him across her desk, 'what do you want to talk about?'

The solid timber chair creaked as he sat.

'You.' Raising his coffee, he drank, watching her all the while. Liar, she thought again, stemming the race of her pulse at the flat statement. He wanted to peer inside her head—know what she knew. That was all.

'What exactly would you like to know, Mr McKay?' She leaned forward, put her elbows on the desk and mockingly made a steeple of her fingers. An appreciate gleam lurked in his eyes as he pulled his chair closer to the desk.

'Some I already know. You're beautiful, independent, tough—though not as tough as you think.'

She studied him carefully, assumed a smug smile. 'I made you leave those trees where they are.'

He blinked at that 'made'. McKay would not care to let anyone think they'd forced him into anything, she was sure. But he gave a sigh and a rueful grin.

'So you did.'

Baloney, she thought. He'd capitulated for reasons of his own, not because of anything she'd done.

'So I must be tough, Mr McKay, mustn't I?' she pressed, 'to take on the shrewd, dynamic Cort McKay that the finance mags are always on about—and win?'

'You read finance magazines?' he enquired, looking around. 'I wouldn't have thought in your business it would be necessary.'

'Of course I read them,' she chided. 'I wouldn't want to be caught out by a takeover bid. Murdoch is rumoured to be looking for a new music arm . . .'

He laughed. 'ABBY'S MUSIC FIGHTS MURDOCH BID—that could be front-page stuff.'

She smiled too, fascinated by the warmth he generated with his smile. What a hell of an act this was. She was intrigued to see how far he would take it to pump her.

'The dangers of takeover wouldn't be a joke to TITAN, I imagine.'

'No. In fact I was only saying the other day—a bid by Adsteam would just about round out our present platterful of problems.'

'Not in financial straits, Mr McKay, surely?'

'Not at present. But the unions have been diabolical this year—and A.W.E. has stopped work at Grady Hill.'

'Life's tough for the mega-companies these days.' She shook her head in mock commiseration. He grinned.

'But good often comes out of bad, I always say——'

'Every cloud has a silver lining?'

'—the dullest morn often heralds in the fairest day——'

'Is that a cliche or a quote?'

'—without the A.W.E. I wouldn't have met you.'

Oh boy. She'd actually felt a thrill up her spine at that sexy voice, those flattering words. What a pity they weren't true.

'You might regret that you ever did,' she said levelly.

'Why do you say that?'

'Who knows——' she shrugged. 'We might find something on yet another of your sites to campaign against—or for. You wouldn't like that I'm sure.'

He tensed a bit. 'No. I wouldn't.'

'You've come to terms with your union problems I hear—what will you do about the A.W.E., Mr McKay? You did say you let nothing stand in your way.'

'Ah, but you've scored two victories, Abby—you're not going to bother us again, are you?'

It was a statement but the question was in his eyes. Abby sat back in her chair and simply smiled. Just what was on that island?

Cort took his coffee-cup over to the minuscule sink and rinsed it.

'There's a pizza place a few doors down. Why not have dinner with me?'

'Pizza?' she said. 'You sent Guerlain perfume to persuade me to eat pizza with you? Overkill, isn't it?'

'I did have something more elaborate in mind. But I've got you here and I know you haven't eaten yet. I have an hour or so to spare before I get back to my desk. So how about it?'

'You haven't "got me here",' she said rather sharply, homing in on the phrase.

'Haven't I?' He leaned near the top of the stairs. 'You can't get down without getting past me.'

'You wouldn't use brute force, Mr McKay——'

'Oh, I don't know. It might be fun.'

'It wouldn't be. As you've pointed out, I'm a big girl.'

'I'm bigger.'

There was no refuting that. Cort McKay looked almost indolent as he leaned there—but the laziness was sheer confidence. Physically he could outmatch her with ease. He was probably only baiting her but Abby was not anxious to call his bluff. She didn't want to feel those large, capable hands on her—the way they had moved on the guitar, all strength yet tenderness . . . she was horrified to feel her face warm up again. Cort watched her with that same odd look he'd had when he'd given her the instrument for tuning.

'So it's pizza or pugilism, Mr McKay?'

'Good God, no—I can think of better ways to use my advantage with a beautiful woman.'

'In that case,' she said drily, 'it definitely will be the pizza.'

The Pizzeria was a tiny place holding a half-dozen tables checkered with cloths. Worn posters of Naples, Rome and Venice hung on the walls. Synthesised mandolins trilled 'Arrivederci Roma'. Abby relaxed and waited for Cort to re-open his subtle enquiries while they drank red wine and waited for their pizza. She felt a great deal safer here than in her office.

But to her surprise he didn't fish any more. Instead he asked her about her music—when she had learned to play, and how. Who was her favourite guitarist? Williams. He had some Williams records—and some of Sky. Where did he live? she asked. Hunters Hill—a view across Lane Cove River towards Tambourine

Bay. He had a catamaran but not much time to take it out. Did she like sailing? Never been. She didn't know what she was missing.

The pizza came and they talked as they ate. With real interest he asked about her business and even his ultra-professional questions about her finance and lease arrangements did not jar.

'Do you plan on expanding your business, Abby?'

'Not just yet. I know how to run a small business. If I change my operation I could find myself working beyond my capacity—financially and in the administrative sense.'

'Smart.' He nodded. 'A lot of small businesses fail because people don't see that. You've done well. How come your parents don't approve of you?'

It was tossed in so carelessly, muted by mandolins and red wine and Abby looked up, eyes vulnerable for a second.

'I heard you talking on the phone,' he said.

'Did you have to eavesdrop?'

'I found out quite a bit about you from that phone conversation,' he said, unashamed. 'How old you are—your parents' disapproval. Why do they disapprove?'

'My parents are academics—I broke from family tradition. And the least I could have done if I was to shun education was to help population. Commerce is not a good enough alternative to either.'

'Does it bother you?'

'I'm twenty-six as you overheard. Parental approval has come my way rarely—I've grown used to it. And you, Mr McKay—do your parents approve of you?'

He grimaced. 'Hell no. Dad never got over his disappointment that I lost my north-country accent at the posh school he sent me to—and he's not convinced that I can run a business properly. And my mother——' he sighed. 'My mother thinks I work too hard, don't eat the proper food and fail to wear my warm undies in winter.'

'And is she right?' Abby smiled, won from her annoyance by his artlessness.

'On at least one count.'

She eyed the pizza. 'Diet or overwork?'

'Neither of those.' He grinned. 'Warm undies are so unsexy.'

Abby giggled, caught back the sound and pushed her wine glass away.

'Do your parents live here or in England?'

'England. Near York. They visited once. Loved the sun and the harbour—hated the pubs. "Nowt like pubs back 'ome, lad",' Cort drawled in imitation. His eyes crinkled up in a smile as she laughed again. He was excellent company. Funny and—nice. But of course he was working at it. Abby was surprised to realise that she'd forgotten that for a while. She ate her last scrap of pizza and dabbed her mouth with the napkin.

'That was quite pleasant, Mr McKay. Did you find out what you wanted?'

'Find out?'

'You wanted to talk about me—wasn't that the object of calling on me this evening?'

He leaned back in his chair. 'There are a few things I'd still like to know. What makes you cry, what books you read. Whether flowers make you sneeze——'

Ridiculous. He was making her smile again.

'—what you look like first thing in the morning——'

The words created a clear, bright image. His raven head on a pillow next to her. Opening her eyes to find him awake, smiling at her . . .

'That will have to remain a mystery, won't it?' she said and looked at her watch, knowing well that she looked on the defensive. But he said nothing—raised a hand and brought the waiter running with the bill.

They went back to the shop. Abby felt nervous again away from the canned mandolins and Italian kitchen chatter. It was a long time since a man had made her nervous. A long time.

'Don't bother with all the lights,' Cort said and went by the glow of the display window to fetch his guitar. 'Is your car parked out back?' At her nod, he said, 'Then I'll see you to it.'

'No need. I often leave later than this alone.'

'After you,' he said as if she hadn't spoken and gestured towards the back exit. Abby opened her mouth to argue, anxious only to get rid of him now. Back here he seemed no longer funny and nice. In the confines of the shadowed shop he was a looming, powerful figure sending out vibrations that were almost audible. Like the hum of a guitar string long after its note had sounded.

The street light and the window spot combined to send the shadows of the displayed violin and drum kit streaking across the floor to fall crookedly on Cort. A slash of light illuminated the lower half of his face. The curve of his mouth was clear and though his eyes were shadowed, Abby could see their gleam.

'I don't need an escort,' she said at last.

'You've got one anyway.' He made a small, mock bow and his face dipped briefly into full light. His eyes were amused but keen. He could see her apprehension, she knew.

'Oh, for heaven's sake—if you must cling to some outmoded idea that a woman can't manage to get to a car unaided——' she muttered ungraciously and went past him, more eager than ever to be gone from her place of work that was suddenly charged with atmosphere and intimacy.

She knew the layout like the back of her hand—the position of every display grouping—the sheet-music carousel, the school-band instrument clutter—and in the semi-gloom shot through it all, keys in her hand as if the devil himself pursued her.

'Such haste——' Cort murmured close behind her, 'it's a good thing you know your way——'

Whether it was his voice that made her falter, or whether Helen had made one of her alterations to the displays, Abby misjudged and her shoulder bag flicked at cymbals that should have been out of reach. Their clash jerked her around and her arm, outflung for balance, hit something. Sleigh bells and triangles shivered and rang with premature Christmas festiveness.

'Are you okay?' Cort took her arm. The strong grip, the sudden, solid closeness of him threw her.

'Of course I'm——' she tugged free, stumbled over a flex from one of the Gibson electrics. Her keys, dangling from one hand, performed a delicate arpeggio along a glockenspiel and she fetched up against a drum kit. Her foot landed unerringly on the pedal and the bass drum boomed once. The sound reverberated around the shop.

Cort had an arm around her.

'She shall have music wherever she goes,' he murmured and hitched her close against him. As he folded his other arm about her, she felt the brush of the guitar he was still holding. 'Stand still before you turn into a symphony orchestra. Why the panic, Abby?' he asked in the same low tone.

'Panic?' she tried to say lightly. 'Don't be silly. I just tripped. Helen must have moved something...' He stirred against her, angling his head to hers and the darkness closed in, seemed to push them together.

'Does your pulse always run at that rate?' he asked,

as her heart slammed away in top tempo against his chest.

'What rate?' she said and tried to pull away. He held her there, moved his foot to the drum pedal. The bass boomed out in perfect rhythm with her heartbeat. It stilled Abby, almost shocked her—to hear her own reaction to him translated into music of a kind. The shop shook to her heartbeat.

'Stop it,' she cried, and he did.

There was silence. Cort leaned close again.

'Let me go,' she said abruptly and after a moment he complied. Carefully, very carefully, she traversed the remaining distance to the back door, fighting hard to recover her equilibrium.

'Your pulse rate would go up too if you thought you might damage valuable stock. That drum kit is already sold and the buyer is picking it up tomorrow——'

But Cort wasn't fooled. Outside as she locked the door, he said,

'I wasn't going to kiss you, you know. I'm old fashioned about that too. Never try it on the first date.'

Abby doubted that. Turning she found him quite close—the guitar hitched under one arm. There was a mingle of moonlight and streetlight slanting on to his craggy face.

'But I'm tempted to make an exception——' he murmured and in slow motion leaned forward. Abby stood mesmerised until his lips were almost touching hers. Then she ducked sideways and fumbled her car key from the others on the ring.

'It's a good rule. Don't break it,' she advised. 'And don't get mugged going to your car, Mr McKay. I'd hate to see you lose your guitar before you've had time to play it.'

Some joke. It would be a brave mugger who took

him on. He chuckled. As she reversed out into the
service lane, he waited—a formidable figure in the
headlights. He had the guitar in front of him. Both
arms were wrapped, loverlike, around it.

Marlene sighed at the heap of notes and scrawled
letters that Cort had turned out the night before. He
had left before she had, but obviously must have
returned to the office later. She had them sorted into
piles when her boss's voice growled through the
Intercom.

'Marlene, get me some coffee, will you?'

When she went in with it, Cort was frowning over a
bundle of files that she recognised as the island project
paperwork. He looked broodingly at her as she set the
coffee down, not really seeing her at all.

'Mr Conrad rang,' she said. 'He wants to make an
appointment with you to introduce their new junior
partner.'

Conrad, Chapman and Connors were TITAN's
legal representatives and the subject of an ongoing
joke between Marlene and Cort. They maintained that
only those whose names commenced with 'C' were
ever considered for higher things in the firm of
Conrad, Chapman and Connors.

Cort's eyes crinkled. 'Not another "C"?'

'Yep,' she grinned. 'Castle, would you believe.'

The silly joke banished Cort's frown.

'How would you like to spend a few days on the
island, Marlene, when work starts there?'

Her grey eyes widened. 'You wouldn't be fooling,
would you, Cort? You wouldn't be that cruel.'

'I'm serious. Do you think Charlie and the kids
could get along without you while you set up a site
office for me?'

'I'll make sure of it.' Marlene hesitated. 'Do you

suspect there will be any delays? I mean—the
A.W.E.—are they likely to make any more trouble?'

'I won't let anything delay it, Marlene. I've worked
too long on it to allow a bunch of women to hold us
up.'

'Do they know about it then?'

'It's possible.' Cort drank some coffee and lowered
his eyes to the files again. 'But I know a way to find
out for certain,' he added roughly.

Turning to go, Marlene saw the covered guitar
against the wall.

'Is this yours, Cort?' she exclaimed and his dark
head lifted.

'Yes.'

The tone brooked no further discussion. Marlene
glanced from him to the instrument as she went out. A
smile moved her mouth as she shut the door. For she
had seen the sticker on the guitar cover. ABBY'S
MUSIC. So, she thought triumphantly, Cort had
wasted no time in following up the tall redhead. Never
mind his reasons—he probably wasn't sure about them
himself. Her husband had guffawed and told her she
was crazy when she had predicted that Abby Milburn
and Cort McKay could well be a perfect match.

'On the strength of one meeting when they
exchanged insults?' Charlie had snorted, 'You women
are amazing. How you can spot a romance in that I
don't know.'

But Charlie hadn't seen the current flow between
the two. She flipped through her floppy disks file.
Wait till she told Charlie that her boss had already
called on the lady in question. And bought a guitar
from her as well ... it was going to be very
interesting.

'Oh, you sold a guitar!' Helen exclaimed at the empty

space on the shop's wall. 'An expensive one too. Who bought it?'

'For heaven's sake Helen, I don't get the names of everyone who buys something,' Abby said irritably.

'You do when they buy guitars,' Helen pointed out with a wounded look. 'For the free lessons.'

Abby's Music offered three free lessons with the purchase of every guitar. In Cort McKay's case, Abby had made an exception.

'This was someone from the country,' she said lamely, avoiding Helen's eyes. Thank goodness Cort hadn't come into the shop while her assistant was here. She would be positively quivering with speculation.

The empty patch drew Abby's gaze again and again that day. Three days, she thought uneasily. It was just three days since the man had loomed up in her life and already he was creating empty spaces. Before she went home that night she fetched a banjo and fitted it on the brackets to fill the gap Cort McKay had made.

As she cooked her meal back in her apartment, her thoughts returned to last night—the rich timbre of his laughter when she had admitted her inability to throw him out, his mock offence when she questioned his prowess on the guitar. His revelation of himself as a nagged, fussed-over son. He was likeable some of the time. Abby dumped two charred lamb chops on to her plate and scowled, recalling that drumbeat in her shop. He was dangerous. All the time.

When the telephone rang she almost didn't answer it. She must have known.

'Evening, Abby.'

'Mr McKay.'

'Call me Cort.' His clipped speech was a trifle slower—his deep voice grained, sexy. Abby fancied she could hear a touch of the north in some of his vowels tonight. It was earthy, attractive. Maybe, she thought as the ground shifted beneath her again, if she told him she only had the merest hint of Paradise and didn't intend to do anything about it, he would leave her alone. Her conscience tweaked. But as a member, and spokesperson of A.W.E., shouldn't she do something?

'No. What's on your mind, Mr McKay?'

'I want to know when I'll get my free guitar lessons. You have a notice in your window offering three with the purchase of every instrument and I consider it very shabby that you didn't tell me about it.'

'Oh, didn't I mention that?' she prevaricated, grimacing at the idea of being cooped up in the tiny studio or the shop with big, vibrant Cort McKay for three half-hour stints. And she could hardly let Paul Donaldson teach him. The young man's nerves would be stretched to the limit. 'I thought you said you could already play.'

'Of course I can play,' he assured her. 'But I need some help with technique, Abby.'

Oh no you don't, she thought. No help at all.

'My student timetable is in my office, Mr McKay, so I'll have to let you know when I can fit you in.'

Why had she got involved like this? Now he had a cast-iron excuse to follow her up. She should never have sold him the guitar. Should have thrown him out of the shop. An exasperated laugh broke from her at the idea. Like trying to shift Ayers Rock.

'Will you be at this meeting you've forced me into, Abby?'

'Forced? You could always cancel,' she said hopefully. 'I'm sure the committee would understand.'

Abby wished devoutly she hadn't pushed him into it. At the time it had seemed only fair after all his innuendoes. But that was days ago and now—now she wanted to keep some distance between herself and Mr McKay.

'You'd like that, wouldn't you?' He sounded amused. 'Why do you keep backing off from me?'

'I don't know what you mean.'

'For such a militant lady you're damned shy—I have only to touch you or look as if I might, for you to put on your armour. Take last night for instance—you blundered around your shop as if you were being pursued.'

'I told you, I tripped——'

'Hmmph. It was the most—musical exit I've heard. The only instruments you didn't accidentally play were the trumpets and the violins.'

'Very amusing, Mr McKay. I hope you intend to tell us all about TITAN's plans for Grady Hill at our meeting.'

'Back to business eh, Abby? In full armour and in full retreat. I really am intrigued to know why I scare you so.'

'Perhaps I just don't like you, have you thought of that?'

'It never crossed my mind,' he said cheerfully.

'Let it,' she urged.

He chuckled. 'Tell me one thing—do flowers make you sneeze?'

There he was, doing it again—making her smile, making her like him in spite of all that she said.

'Good night, Mr McKay.' She hung up.

Looking around her comfortable flat, Abby wondered why she was no longer at peace. Her married friends envied her freedom, her success. She worked for herself in a field of her own choosing, lived well in this old but stylish apartment. Everything around her was there by choice, selected with care and immense pleasure. Blatantly modern and stately old chairs sat in harmony around a small Persian rug. Her pictures and treasured small ornaments were displayed on the walls and surfaces and books filled several shelves. A Greek bouzouki and two guitars hung above her divan, their honeyed tones gleaming warmly in the lamplight. Abby sighed, went to close the curtains.

Her life was just the way she wanted. She had Martin, a good friend more than a boyfriend and never a lover—but an intelligent, warm man she valued. Martin was seven years older than her but greying prematurely towards middle age. He made her laugh. He was uncomplicated, undemanding. Martin went with her comfortable, interesting, rewarding life.

She paced back and forth across the Persian rug and knew that her restlessness could be traced back to one person.

CHAPTER FOUR

THE A.W.E. Committee seemed sceptical about Abby's story of the proposed job on Paradise. Her own sketchy details did make it seem rather lacklustre, but she felt impelled to tell them anyway.

'I think it is why Mr McKay succumbed so quickly over the Winston trees and why he offered to speak at the next general meeting. To get us off his back—and maybe head us off before we found out anything . . .'

But A.W.E. preferred issues that were clear cut. It was really rather funny, Abby thought. Mr McKay might be launching his campaign on her for no reason at all. Nevertheless, she contacted a few of her parents' university colleagues on the chance that an independent wildlife survey might have been done on Paradise. In the end she was referred to a John Mansfield who had been approached to do some studies in the subtropics. His wife informed Abby that he had not in fact taken the work, that he was currently away and she would get him to phone her on his return.

Abby hadn't received a call from him by Wednesday, the day of the A.W.E. meeting. What she did receive at the shop, before the interested gaze of two customers and Helen, was an enormous box of roses. White roses—exquisite, long-stemmed—expensive. Abby's heart thumped as she ripped open the envelope of the accompanying card. She knew who had sent them before she read the one word written boldly within the gilt edge . . . *Gesundheit.*

'Ooh, they're lovely!' Helen cried and her look at

64

Abby was one big question. It was clear that she had arrived at the correct conclusion when she failed to ask who had sent them. Abby turned the small card absently between her fingers. Perfume—now flowers. He was crowding her. She smiled at the ridiculous single word on the card, then crushed the square of cardboard, and hurried to attend her customers. While she slipped music books into a bag and gave change, the heady perfume of Cort McKay's roses lingered in her nostrils.

The meeting was held in a church hall that was tucked away in a lane high over Middle Harbour and reached via a network of steep streets. Rows of stackable metal chairs filled fast and Abby stepped outside to the hall's side stair landing for a few breaths of cold air. Joel Hamilton followed her and she turned from her absent study of the ink and silver harbour glimpses to find his admiring eyes on her.

'Beautiful night,' he said. 'Beautiful spokesperson.'

'Mr Hamilton,' she put out her hand to him, 'have they spared you from the sports pages again?'

'I see you didn't like my piece about you and Cort,' he grinned and hitched his camera strap around his neck. 'But you came out of it very well.'

'With a bit too much embellishment. I wish you'd just report my quotes on behalf of A.W.E. Whether I'm a "striking redhead" or not is really irrelevant.'

'You'll see, Abby—your looks will get A.W.E. more publicity than it ever could with just good works. You're going to be a celebrity.'

She made an impatient sound. 'Titan and the Amazon, for heaven's sake. You made us sound like one of the sporting events you should be covering— and in this corner, the brawny brawler from Great Britain, Titan himself versus——'

'Hey now, that's not a bad idea——'

'Mr Hamilton,' she said warningly. But he assured her it was a joke.

'My editor liked that piece of mine—and the photo. Said he could almost feel the vibrations between you and Cort.'

She stared at him, uneasy at his bracketing of them together. There was a wearily amused look about his eyes that was likeable—a shabby, scruffy sort of charm in his brown clothes and ruffled greying hair.

'I *wish* you'd go back to sports.'

'Got to finish covering this wrestling match first. I'm hanging on for the final clinch, you see.'

Abby bristled but before she could rebuke him, she turned her head and saw Cort coming up the steps. Joel Hamilton looked from one to the other intently. Cort greeted him then concentrated on Abby.

'Did they make you sneeze?' he asked as he came up the last step to crowd the small landing.

'No,' she snapped, unwilling to get involved in his baiting in front of the newsman.

'White roses seemed right. Yellow were too insipid, pink too frivolous, red——' he pursed his mouth, '—perhaps too full-blooded yet. White was the perfect foil for hair like yours, Abby.' The deep voice was edged with humour. He was quite calculatingly hinting at a closer relationship for Hamilton's benefit.

'Let's hope they're the perfect foil for the waste-bin then, Mr McKay, because that's where I put them,' she said tartly and moved inside, followed by the two men.

His address, if it could be called that, was an education. There was more than a touch of the English north in his voice tonight. The clipped vowels and sharp consonants were longer, less defined. Subtly it created a cosier air—a confiding air. The amiable giant from the provinces. Ha! Abby thought. That harmless, palatable accent had belonged to other hard-nosed men who had founded vast industrial empires.

He astonished the gathering by telling them that TITAN was looking at a design change for Grady Hill.

'Experts have found traces of other early buildings nearby—quarry labourers' cottages in all likelihood. TITAN proposes to build replicas of the church and those cottages and make design alterations in the complex to complement their Georgian/colonial characteristics. The replicas will be leased out to suitable craft groups and guilds to enhance the village flavour we hope to create. Convict bricks found on the site will be incorporated into the church building and a plaque inserted to commemorate those early builders —one of whom, as I told Miss Milburn recently, could well have been an ancestor of mine who came out here on government assistance, you might say——'

It was received with laughter and applause. Abby was pleased. TITAN was not entirely insensitive to history or the environment after all. This marriage of the past and the present was exactly the kind of development that would enrich rather than enrage future generations. But as she clapped, she couldn't help wondering if this announcement was serving a double purpose. A.W.E. certainly approved of TITAN now. Mr McKay could confidently expect them to leave him alone.

Abby watched him, seeing the solid core of energy, his ambition, determination. And every now and then the boyish smile would light those craggy features. 'I'd like to know how you look first thing in the morning——' What would he look like first thing in the morning? But when her mind leapt ahead of the question she cut short the wondering.

An education. But what she was learning bothered

her. Cort McKay, so much a man she should dislike, was a man she could like too much. The deep well of humour behind his smile, the controlled dynamism that moved his large hands in sweeping arcs of pure energy, his visual impact. Abby hardly heard what he said.

She admitted that she was strongly attracted to him. It was the first time in years—since Simon—that she had felt so physically drawn to anyone. Not just physical, she corrected. Cort's eyes dropped to hers as if he was tuned in to her. Then he went on, a warm change in his voice that told Abby he had glimpsed something of her thoughts in her face.

Question time and Cort played off the ladies' queries smoothly. There was no sting in them now that Grady Hill had established his bona fides.

'Let's leave the city for the moment,' Abby said. 'You've built condominiums on the central coast and I imagine you plan more of this entrepreneurial investment. When you build in previously undeveloped areas, does TITAN institute safeguards—geological, environmental and wildlife studies——?'

'Of course.'

'And those surveys are made available for public scrutiny?'

'It isn't always obligatory.'

'And perhaps not always desirable for TITAN. Especially if the project was being kept secret for—oh, let's say, financial reasons.'

'Secret, Abby?' he smiled. Warily. She ploughed on, choosing her words with care to intimate greater knowledge than she had to try and put him on the spot. But she was well aware there was little chance of succeeding.

As before though, success came all too easily. Cort put up a hand and ran it over his jet-dark hair. He shifted his weight from one foot to the other. The picture of a man making up his mind. Abby frowned.

'Well, Abby, you would have heard about it eventually anyway, but as you've got me wiggling on a hook I suppose I'll have to tell you now——' He gave a resigned shrug. 'Yes, it's true we've kept our holiday complex under wraps because it is a year away from a final concept——'

She blinked, not believing this! On a hook—Cort McKay!

'—situated on Queensland's north coast and will entail I admit the clearing of some rainforest land——' there was a murmur from the audience and he held up his hands. 'However, I'm sure when you hear our safeguards . . .'

Such devastating honesty. Abby smiled. What a consummate actor he was. Add that to the bewildering array of Cort McKay's abilities. Such sporting good humour at being found out. The man had actually let her bait him so that he was 'forced' to confess. But wily Mr McKay was confessing to something else. The job he wanted to hide was not *on* the Queensland coast, but *off* it. Right smack in the resort belt of the Great Barrier Reef. This was a red herring. It was swallowed willingly by his audience. He gathered up his notes and after Iris's official thanks and applause, he left the stage and made for Abby.

'Your father would have been proud of you tonight, Mr McKay.'

'Why is that, Abby?'

'That posh school didn't entirely smother your origins. Such a nice *countrified* sound, your accent. I really had to push myself to remember I was listening to tough, shrewd dynamo Cort McKay.'

'Ee lass, did tha' like it?' he grinned.

The camera's flash caught them and Abby turned

away. After much informal discussion the meeting broke up and she waited ten minutes after Cort had dragged himself away from the animated A.W.E. members before she walked down the steep road to her car. What now, she mused. He had shrewdly diverted their attention to another supposed 'secret' when she pressed him. But he must be aware by the nature of her questions that her earlier references to Paradise weren't accidental. *She* was the fly in the ointment, for Cort must know that she was not fooled by his confession. So what would he do about her—more flowers and flattery? Would he continue to pursue her? Suddenly Abby felt deflated. What would it be like if he was doing all that and there was no island project—no ulterior motives? 'Fool,' she muttered and stooped to insert her key in the car door.

'Now that's what I call a view.' The lazy voice from behind startled Abby, made her drop the keys. She bent to retrieve them and slowly turned. Cort raised his eyes from her rear.

'Still here, Mr McKay? You left a good ten minutes ago. Trouble with your car?' she tacked on hopefully.

He laughed and the sound was resonant, pleasing. It was a sound that would be good to hear on a winter's night in front of a fire. Or first thing in the morning . . .

'No trouble. You took your time. Or was brave Abby making sure I'd be gone before she ventured out?' he mocked.

'Have you been waiting for me?' she demanded. He would have recognised her car from the night at the shop.

'Don't men always wait for you?'

'Not men like you.'

'What men am I like?'

She swallowed. The fact was he didn't quite fit into

any category. She'd never met a man like him.

'Busy men, ambitious men—men preoccupied with making and keeping their empires before anything else.'

'There are other things on my mind right now.'

He moved closer and she saw the teasing smile that softened his hard mouth, the glint in his eyes. His large frame was silvered by moonlight and set against the Mondrian squares of light—windows lit brightly from within or palely by the moon from without. A gold square, a red. Houses, terraced and tiered, over-lapped each other on their way up the steep slope and made a black-and-grey glittering backdrop to Cort.

'Your holiday resort on the north Queensland coast, for instance?' she asked sardonically.

'You had me in a corner, Abby—all those questions. You just prised it out of me.'

'You know very well you've given us no victory— my questions were aimed at——' Paradise Island, she almost said and stopped. After his announcement about Grady Hill and his seeming open-book attitude on the resort, A.W.E. were no longer interested. So she might as well keep her suspicions to herself. If Cort felt he was really off the hook now maybe he would leave her alone.

'Yes?' he prompted.

'—aimed at general matters,' she said weakly. 'You only told us what you did because it suited you. I don't overestimate our power, Mr McKay.'

'You're underestimating your own, though. I nearly forgot my speech tonight when you looked at me with that smile in your eyes——'

His voice was a velvet-soft stroke. The man was an arm's length from her yet she could almost feel his touch.

'You imagined it.'

'No.' Cort raised his arm and she leaned back against her car. But his hand found the decided edge of her jaw, curved to cover her cheek and the shadowed indent of her neck. As she froze, he drew his hand forward until only his thumb and fingertips touched her chin. It was the way he had caressed the guitar and Abby felt the music deep inside her. His voice dropped lower still.

'We could stretch a point and regard this as a second date,' he murmured and stepped suddenly close before she could move. There was a brief sensation of being surrounded—of the warmth and solid strength of his chest beneath her defensive hands. His mouth touched hers. If earlier she had wondered how it would be with him, it was not like this. A light, tender touch of his lips, withdrawn then repeated with more deliberation but the same sweet lack of demand. The kind of kiss she'd dreamed about at sixteen before she discovered the reality was uncontrolled, wet and unromantic. Abby could have fought against his passion but she was momentarily disarmed by his tenderness. When he stepped away and the cool air rushed around her, she knew herself more threatened than ever.

'Good night Abby,' he said softly and walked away.

The scent of his roses was a fragrant mockery as she opened the door of her flat. She threw off her jacket and went to stroke the petals of one of the white blooms. Why on earth hadn't she just thrown the flowers in the waste bin?

Abby cursed her loose tongue when she saw Hamilton's piece on the A.W.E. meeting the next day. 'McKAY v. MILBURN' he'd headed it as if it was a wrestling match. His photograph featured Abby and Cort, eyes locked. Again. 'The battle of the giants is still on, with A.W.E. the winner again——' he'd written and gone on to the revelations about Grady Hill and the northern resort. There were a few totally irrelevant details about Abby including a mention of her music shop and a flattering description: 'Miss Milburn is a tall, beautiful redhead and possibly a thorn in Cort McKay's side. Maybe that's why he sends her roses. Then again—maybe not.'

A week later the TITAN boss had made no further enquiries about guitar lessons and Abby came to the conclusion that it had been merely an 'open door' tactic in reserve had he needed to keep up his pursuit. On reflection, he must have decided that A.W.E.—and she herself—no longer represented a threat. And that was just fine, she told herself. She was glad the reporter's hints of a burgeoning relationship were proved wrong. The roses died and she threw them out.

But Joel Hamilton had been right about one thing, she discovered. She had become something of a celebrity. Astonishing amounts of mail began arriving at the shop, the name of which had been included in the news piece. Most of the letters were supportive or congratulatory about Winston or Grady Hill, some were rude and one was amusingly Victorian in tone, imploring her to give up her jeans and hoydenish ways and act like a lady. It might almost have come from the pen of her mother, except that it contained a spelling error. The letters all had one thing in common. They began 'Dear Abby' as if each writer fancied his or her own wit and originality. To Abby it was something of a joke, but Helen revelled in it and gave the letter opening priority over even her dedicated reorganisation of the displays. Martin called in after closing one night, equally intrigued.

'How many today?' he enquired, his jaws moving as

he chewed. It always amused Abby that Martin, almost a father figure in looks, chewed gum which gave an odd incongruity to his appearance, and churned out his words with many a juice consonant. Gum had taken the place of cigarettes when he'd given up smoking a few months ago and, Abby chided him, he was hooked all over again. 'Better a chain-chewer than a chain-smoker,' he told her. 'At least that's what my doctor tells me.'

At the sight of the pile of mail, a low whistle halted the movement of his jaws. '*That* many? Okay, let's have a look at this batch of "Dear Abby" letters.' They began opening those reluctantly left by Helen. 'Aha—here's an offer you can't refuse. A proposal.' Martin's grey eyes crinkled in amusement as he laid the letter on the counter.

'Of marriage?'

'Certainly, certainly. The gentleman lists quite frankly all your attributes and his own and concludes that you and he are a perfect match.' Abby scanned the sheet and dropped it in the bin before opening another envelope.

'I can't understand it, Martin. Why do people write to complete strangers just because of a little media——' She stopped abruptly, her face sobering. 'What do you make of this?' She held out a letter to him. It was nasty. While some had been criticising her for standing in the way of progress, this one threatened. '—women who go around poking their noses into things might end up with acid in their faces.'

'A crank, Abby.' Martin read it again, chewing with great concentration. 'I had a feeling you'd get at least one like this. There are always some odd-bods around who enjoy this sort of thing. Leave it with me. I'll drop in and see Bill about it.' Bill Salford was Martin's brother and a plain-clothes detective. 'I don't really think you need to worry. It finishes, "Yours sincerely—A Friend." It's almost funny, isn't it?'

After a day or two when Bill Salford confirmed his opinion she put it out of her mind. But the Dear Abby letters weren't the only result of her two exposures in the press. A magazine invited her to model fashions for tall women and she was asked to record a short segment for a current affairs show and form part of a panel with Cort McKay on one scheduled for a later date. As the A.W.E. spokesperson she had to agree. There were calls from advertising agencies with so-called 'environment-related' products for her endorsement, all of which she refused. The Winston trees and the Grady Hill Village were given a feature in several television programs and somewhere in all of them Abby's name came up. A variety show compere used her name—'I thought I might go and knock off a few whales. Who knows I might get lucky—Abby Milburn might try to talk me out of it——' He leered at the camera.

A.W.E., not altogether approving of the type of publicity she was receiving, nevertheless took full advantage of it. They began to gather more supporters, drew up petitions to present to M.P.s while the spotlight was on them. Abby wondered what Cort McKay made of all this attention they were getting. TITAN was sharing the limelight of course, in its new role of protector. Was it bothering the big man that in the middle of it all she might suddenly drop a bombshell about his island?

The magazine layout was more of a hassle than she expected. She tried on piles of clothes before the Fashion Editor selected three outfits inspired by the Daintree rainforest—then posed for the pictures among the Winston trees. It was the current affairs interview that turned out unexpectedly. The inter-

viewer knew about her fan mail and the anonymous
letter. Helen must have told someone, she supposed.
Her assistant had handled a great many of what she
termed 'media' calls. He broached the subject sidelong,
mentioned the threat and asked if McKay sent her
letters as well as flowers. The inference was clear.

'Have you met Cort McKay, Mr Wiley?'

'Yes, I have.'

'Then I'm surprised you'd even hint at any
connection between him and an anonymous letter.
That's not his style at all.'

When Abby saw herself on screen, stoutly upholding
McKay's reputation, she was more confused than
ever. Somehow she thought the piece would be cut
before it went to air. Martin watched the programme
with her.

'Do you like him?' he asked on a curious note.

'He has certain qualities I suppose—one thing is
certain, Mr McKay is a whole lot less obvious than a
poison-pen type. Wiley could be sued I should think
for hinting such a thing.'

'Mmmm.' Martin eyed her faintly flushed cheeks
and after a moment removed the chewing gum from
his mouth to look at it with dissatisfaction. 'I'd give a
lot for a cigarette.'

Abby hardly heard him. What would Cort think
about this? Damn the media. All that rubbish about a
love/hate relationship and flowers made a perfectly
just and logical statement seem personal.

She found out what Cort thought about it sooner
than she expected, for the next night he called on her
again, at home this time. Her takeaway Chinese meal
finished, Abby had given herself the luxury of a deep
bath and slipped into a favourite white robe. Barney
Kessel's jazz guitar flowed from the stereo as she went
to answer the door.

'Coming,' she called. It didn't occur to her to check who it was. Martin had half promised to call in for a game of chess and though it was a little early she was sure it was him.

But it wasn't. It was Cort dressed for the city in a three-piece suit and striped business shirt and tie. Ultra-civilised clothes that heightened his aggressive masculine looks. Abby was at once burningly conscious that the robe was all she wore and that she was bare-footed. Her head had to tilt a little more to meet his eyes.

'Oh——' she was at a loss momentarily.

'Evening, Abby.' He let his eyes wander over her body, accurately moulded by the clinging silk.

'What is it you want this time, Mr McKay?'

'Hmmm—I'm not sure I should tell you that . . .' Another warm appraisal.

'Fine. In that case——' she made to close the door. With one hand against it, he held it there.

'Invite me in, Abby?' Gently he pushed so that the door swung back further but he didn't come in. It was some sort of moral code, she supposed, that he would use force to prevent her shutting him out, but required an invitation to actually step inside. Abby gave a sigh of exasperation and stepped back. He wasn't going to move, it seemed, and she saw no advantage in a prolonged argument over it. With an exaggerated gesture she waved him in.

'Please *do* come in, Mr McKay.'

He chuckled as he passed her and she shut the door, considering making an excuse to go and change. Her hands went to her robe, overlapping the edges more securely and tightening her belt. At his amused look, she decided to remain as she was just to prove that he did not make her uneasy.

'I really must move to a place with a security door

and intercom system,' she said. His eyes crinkled further and he looked around the half-lit room while she watched him.

'You have a nice touch in decorating, Abby,' he glanced at the Persian rug. 'I have one of these myself.'

Abby sat down in an armchair. 'I dare say yours is a bit bigger than mine. And I do wish you'd sit down because with you standing on it, my rug is looking smaller by the minute,' she added plaintively. It had been the largest of the beautiful carpets she could afford—with Cort McKay planted on it, it assumed the proportions of a bathmat.

In easy strides he crossed to sit in the chair facing her. How very gracefully he moved, she thought. Like one of the big cats.

'You're making me self-conscious Abby, with all these quips about my size.'

'You—self-conscious? Ha!'

'I used to be. As you were, I imagine. As a schoolboy I was more a geographical feature than a personality. They used to call me Mount McKay.'

A faint smile touched her mouth. It was hard to think of this man ever being hurt by the silly jokes and names that had plagued her own adolescence.

'Yes, I know what you mean. Kids at school called me A-BIG-ail or Maypole Milburn. It seems funny now . . .'

'It's worse for a girl,' Cort nodded. 'Once past the age of wishing to conform I wasn't too bothered. It gives me certain advantages——' he looked wickedly at her, '—like being able to look down on tall, fiery women.'

'Believe me, Mr McKay, you don't have to be tall to do that. I've been looked down on by some men of puny height.'

'Not for long I'll bet,' he smiled.

'No. Not for long.' She smiled back at him.

In the short silence they just looked at each other and Abby realised she was no longer tense. His presence here didn't seem so strange after all, even somehow inevitable. The thought brought with it the firming of her defences and she reminded herself that Cort was here for a reason and none of his charm could conceal that it was a business one.

'Coffee, Mr McKay?'

'Please.' He got up and took off his jacket. Abby looked back. He made an almost piratical figure in shirtsleeves and waistcoat. 'Call me Cort,' he said as he followed her to the kitchen. 'It's short for Cortney.' This was said with a grimace.

'I know. I did my homework, remember? Cortney Alexander. Don't you like your name?' she enquired, switching on the kettle.

'Let's put it this way. It was a good thing I wasn't a delicate lad with blonde curls.'

She laughed at that, picturing what he had been like, with his tough boy's face turning into a tough man's face under a school cap.

'A nice solid sort of name like John or Paul, that's what I would have liked.'

'Why? You were big enough to defend "Cortney" surely.'

'Too big to defend it without earning the reputation of a bully.'

'The gentle giant?'

'Not always,' he admitted. 'I have it on good authority that I'm like a grizzly when I lose my temper.'

'Then I shan't tangle with you, Mr McKay.'

'Call me Cort, please. I feel the draft of disapproval every time you say Mr McKay.'

She laughed. 'Mr McKay, you are a scheming, ruthless and determined man. I could call you Christopher Robin and you would still feel the draft of disapproval as you call it.'

'Cruel,' he grinned. 'I'd be completely dashed now if I didn't know that you admired some of my qualities.'

'What conceit! Name me one of your qualities that I——' she began and remembered the television programme on which she'd upheld his integrity. Cort sunk his hands into his pockets and watched her colour rise. The kettle began to whistle.

'And so publicly admired them too,' he mused.

Abby seized the kettle and poured boiling water on the instant coffee.

'I said what I believed. In spite of everything I couldn't encourage a rumour like that to start. You may be a calculating man in other ways, but I don't see you posting nasty letters to people. Well, not anonymous ones, anyway.' As she reached up to one of the cupboards for the sugar, his hand closed about her wrist. Her eyes shot to him, startled.

'Thank you for believing that—and for saying so.' He was dead serious and she felt oppressed by some deep emotion. To shake it off she shrugged.

'Don't mention it. It must be some piece of woman's intuition that hasn't perished yet.' Once again she tried to move her hand to the shelf but he held her.

'The threat. How serious was it?'

'A crank. Advising me to stop poking my nose into things that don't concern me or I might get acid in my face.'

His hand tightened. 'Have you told the police?'

'Martin—a friend—took the letter to his brother who is in the force. He didn't doubt it was just nuisance value.'

There was a temptation to go on babbling about the
letters with him standing so close and his hand warm
and secure about her wrist. His thumb moved briefly
over the heel of her hand and the tiny caress set her
heart slamming. But he let her go and she took down
the sugar.

'Martin—is he your boyfriend?'

'That's right.' She put the coffee on a tray and took
it to the lounge.

'What is he like? What does he do?'

Sitting down, she leaned over to pass his coffee.

'So curious. Why do you want to know?'

'Sounding out the competition. If I want to replace
him I need to know what I'm up against.'

CHAPTER FIVE

THE tape had stopped and now Abby registered the silence. She sat frozen with the cup still in her outstretched hand and stared at Cort. His light eyes were intent on her—burning on her. Longing filled Abby. Here was a man who fascinated her, annoyed her, drew her admiration and disapproval almost simultaneously—a man whose tough physical appeal and gentle touch melted her insides. Which meant that he was a man who could, if allowed, make her face that one fear she had never conquered. For a long time she had wondered if there would ever be a man who would make her want to do that—and it had to be this one who was hell bent on protecting his business interests. If she fell smitten into his arms, he could forget about Ms Milburn following up on anything she might have stumbled across. He had come out into the open at last, pushed by the mounting publicity she'd had. Slowly she put the coffee down. He'd stepped up his pace because of the television programme next week on which they would both appear. Cort apparently didn't want to take any risks. By next week he planned to have her eating out of his hand—maybe sleeping in his bed. And even with her built-in fear she could easily fall in with his plans. That was what released her anger on herself and on him. Silk swished as she shot from the chair.

'You'll do anything to protect that damned island of yours, won't you? Do you honestly imagine that I'm gullible enough to fall for this expert line—this surfeit of charm and boyish wit?' Abby's voice began to rise.

'Did you think I'd be just too, too flattered to suspect all the sudden interest in my life—the perfume and phone calls, roses and a line in romantic chat that went out with galoshes? Replace Martin! You egotistical, conniving——' She took the belt of her gown in both hands and snapped it tight again.

Cort stood up, hands on hips. 'Why so offended? You're a beautiful woman—I'm a normal man. I'd like to get to know you. I'd like to make love to you——'

'You and I know what you'd really like and I just happen to be a minor goal along the way. But mark this, Mr McKay, you might have put the others off with your clever act the other night, but I don't believe it.' His eyes narrowed at that. 'The northern resort you spoke about is another venture entirely if it exists at all. You have a luxury resort planned for Paradise Island.' His face darkened at her open use of the name. 'You have a helicopter service already in operation and plan to begin building the crew accommodation within weeks if you haven't already started. And I know there is something—some reason for your shunning of publicity. It's something you'd prefer A.W.E. not to know so it concerns the environment. When I find out who surveyed the island's wildlife for you, then I'll know.'

She knew she was a fool to run on like this before she had any real, hard facts but there was a dull ache deep down in her that drove her on, shooting her ammunition at him.

'So you see, Mr McKay, all your efforts to charm me and shut me up were in vain. You hoped to have me wilting in your arms before the television show next week, I suppose.'

'You seem to be obsessed with this island,' he said grimly, not admitting to it even now. 'Are you certain all this publicity and fan-mail hasn't gone to your head? Or is it fear that you *might* wilt in my arms that's prompting this outburst?'

Too near the mark. Abby drew in a sharp breath.

'No, I'm not afraid that I might forget just what your priorities are. You wanted to find out if I knew anything and now you'd like to make sure I keep quiet——' she paused contemptuously. 'So you decided on sex appeal as the answer to your dilemma. Well, I've got news for you. Flaunt your practised charm and your big, strong shoulders all you like. I'm not impressed.'

He moved towards her, his own anger rising, as she tore on scathingly, 'I've dealt with your kind before—ambitious, selfish—you'll have your own way come hell or high water and you'll use whatever means you have to. Maybe I was wrong about that unsigned letter. You're just unprincipled enough to use even those means to get what you want.'

Buttressed by her anger, she quailed nevertheless before his.

'You'll take that back, Abby,' he bit out and reached for her. Proudly she stood her ground at first, but the lightning-blue eyes blazed at her and she backed away, spitting words at him.

'Get out of my home and don't lay so much as a finger on me or I'll bring a charge of assault against you—how would *that* publicity grab you?'

'You vicious tongued——' he grated and caught up with her as she found herself against the wall. He took her by the shoulders and shook her once, mightily—making her hair fly about her face. 'Why the hell did you have to come barging in——' he bit off the words and frowned down at her, his breathing quick and furious. Abby was deafened by her pulse thundering alarm in her ears. Cort gripped her shoulders and she brought up her hands to ward him off.

'Let me go——'

But even as she gasped the words, the pressure of his hands changed and her pulse-beat became tumultuous as she looked up to see him hungrily absorbing the smooth expanse of her skin where the robe had slipped.

'No,' she said and leaned away, hands on his chest, elbows locked, arms straight to create some distance from him. Cort held her there, watching her face as she strained against him.

'For God's sake, Abby,' he said, 'I lost my temper for a minute, that's all—I'm not trying to rape you——'

He inched her towards him and she tried desperately to keep him at arm's length but he finally exerted his strength and her elbows buckled so that she was close in his arms. Red hair flew wildly in his face as she twisted to be free. She kicked her bare feet at his shins and beat powerfully at his arms and back. Not since Simon had a man ever held her against her will—and though Simon had followed up his forcefulness with his sweet, loving lies, she had never forgotten those awful minutes when he had tried to impose his will on hers. Tears of rage and fear stood out on her lashes when Cort released her abruptly.

'Abby——' he said, watching her push back her hair with a shaking hand, cross her robe more firmly over her heaving breasts, 'what the devil are you afraid of——'

She turned away, intending to show him the door, but he caught her wrist and whipped her back into his arms.

'Is it this?' His mouth came down on hers with the question and though he held her forcefully there was nothing rough in his kiss. Her muffled protests died away at his melting persuasion. Her pulse sounded

loud in her ears—became the reverberation of a bass
drum, the way he had played it once before. Cort
pushed a hand into her tangled hair, spread his fingers
to cup the back of her head . . . her mouth opened and
she felt the touch of his tongue . . . through the silk
gown he caressed her, hands slipping, sliding over the
sheer surface, searing her skin beneath. As he bent his
head to the curve of her neck, Abby drove her fingers
into his dark hair and felt a warm rush of desire. She'd
known . . . Cort kissed her shoulder where the robe
slipped downwards . . . she'd known all along it would
come to this . . . he stepped back, nudged the gown
until it slithered from her in a shimmering, white fall
down her arms and over her wrists to hang suspended
from the belt at her waist. Then the touch of his hands
on her midriff, her breasts, was smooth as the fabric
itself and the caress of his tongue and lips a slow,
silken seduction.

The robe rippled to the floor as Cort lifted her into
his arms and walked to her bedroom. There was a
striping of moonlight from the slatted blind and as he
set her down his eyes were highlighted in a pale bar of
light. Silvered blue, hazy, fierce with desire.

'Abby——' he breathed and there was a hoarse note
in his voice and a tremor to the hand that stroked her
moonstreaked body from temple to thigh, 'you're
magnificent——'

Abby reached up, pulled loose the buttons of his
waistcoat and shirt and he discarded both garments,
muttering impatiently as his tie resisted his fingers. It
flicked upwards, catching a slat of light before it sank
to the floor. Cort joined her, his weight pressing her
back into the giving softness of the padded covers, and
her arms went about him in a surge of excitement.
Had she ever felt this way before? Abby couldn't
remember this feeling . . . all the cold, controlled years

rolled away and she was alive, warm—cradling Cort's head at her breast, delighting in touching him, being touched.

Her body stiffened as his hand curved over the mound of her abdomen, moved downwards with feather strokes . . . his intimate touch was electric but her muscles tensed and her need was not enough to release her. Perhaps, she thought hopefully, perhaps now . . . but she grew rigid as Cort stirred and raised his head.

'Abby?' He ran fingertips along her unresponsive arm. Silence. Abby lay frozen. Tears rushed, filled her eyes but didn't fall. She turned her head so that he wouldn't see.

'Abby?' his voice was edgier as he picked up her change of mood. 'Don't you want this as much as I do?'

Other things came back to mind now with the rough demand. His determination to protect his project.

'No—I didn't want it to go this far——'

His recoil was instant. Abby reached for the bedcover's edge and gathered the quilting inadequately about her as Cort stood to pull on his shirt.

'I don't believe that. You were making love to me too as if you expected to take this to its natural conclusion. And you're no blushing schoolgirl—so why call a halt now?'

Because I'm afraid I'll be less than a woman in your arms—because something that promises to be magic might turn to emptiness—because I've discovered I feel something more than want for you and you want me for my silence. She sat up, pulled the cover with her.

'To show you that I could.'

Eyes narrowed, he took a few moments to answer. 'To prove that you were in control—not me?' he said, a little too calmly. 'War games?'

She snatched at it. 'That's right.'

'You were taking one hell of a chance then, Abby.' He knelt on the bed and she used every ounce of muscle-power to stop herself shrinking from him. 'With the encouragement I got, I couldn't be blamed for simply taking what I want.'

She shook her head. 'You wouldn't do that, Cort.' Whatever else he might be, she knew he was not a brute. If only she could view Cort in plain black and white. It was all those grey eyes of his that made it impossible to do the sensible thing and dislike him. 'And I know you couldn't have sent that anonymous letter. I apologise for saying that.'

'You apologise for the letter!' he sneered. 'Well, isn't that just dandy.'

Reaching out he tipped her face to him, angled it until a bar of moonlight lay across her eyes. It caught the sparkle of tears still on her lashes and she squeezed her eyes closed too late.

'Oh don't cry as well,' he said sarcastically. 'After that wrap-up for my morals I'm not likely to leap on you again.'

But in spite of his anger and frustration Abby fancied she saw speculation in his eyes as he searched her face.

'What happened to you, Abby—to scare you so?' he asked in a softer tone. 'Who was he?'

She turned her head away and his hand dropped from her with a last, light brush of his fingers.

'Please go, Cort.'

At the doorway he looked back at her. His waistcoat and tie were slung over one shoulder.

'I've achieved something tonight,' he said with a sardonic twist to his mouth. 'I got you to call me Cort.'

*　　　*　　　*

Marlene beckoned Dave Sinclair to her desk as he headed towards Cort's office the next morning.

'A word of warning,' she said in a low voice. 'He's in a black mood. What on earth's happened?'

Dave squared his shoulders. 'No idea. But I hope I haven't put my foot in anything.'

Marlene was thoughtful. 'He's like a caged lion. Last night when I left the office he was okay. I wonder——' Another trip to visit a redhead? Dave went to the door and knocked.

'Just a simple funeral,' he told Marlene with the face of a martyr. 'No flowers please.'

'Morning, Cort,' Dave said when he was bade to enter.

'Someone must have talked to her about the Paradise job,' Cort growled. 'Any ideas?'

Dave frowned. 'Her? Who, Cort?'

His boss glared. 'Who? Abby Milburn, of course.'

Dave's mouth pursed in a silent whistle.

'Find out how she knew. I've got to appear on a television show with her next week and she's likely to blurt the damned lot out.'

'I don't see how knowing her source will help you there, Cort.'

Cort looked stonily at him. 'I want to know.'

It was just after midday when Paul Donaldson, pale and shaken, walked into ABBY'S MUSIC. Helen gave him a curious look as she went to lunch and Abby felt the stirrings of disaster.

'I've been sacked,' Paul told her and sat down to lay the whole thing squarely at her feet. The TITAN boss had accused Paul of spying for Abby, given him a tongue-lashing that had him trembling still and refused him any references. As Paul had worked for

TITAN since he left school, that was a severe
punishment.

'Mr Sinclair came down to see me—he'd been
asking around and wanted to know if it was true that I
worked part-time for you and the next thing I knew I
was in the Managing Director's office and . . .' he
shook his head. 'I can't understand what set it all
off.'

Abby could. She lashed herself for throwing her
knowledge of Paradise prematurely at Cort. That was
what had prompted him to look for a leak in TITAN.
Guiltily she patted Paul's arm and her depression
deepened. The morning had been a strain even
without this drama. Sleep had been slow to come after
Cort left her last night.

'How am I going to tell Jill—in her condition?' Paul
said.

'Look, I'll go and see Mr McKay, Paul. Perhaps I
can convince him that you weren't to blame.' Her face
paled at the prospect of facing a raging Cort who
thought she'd planted a spy on him. But Paul's
hopeful face made her feel guiltier than ever. 'I'll go as
soon as Helen gets back from lunch. You go home and
I'll phone you there.'

Cort was out but expected back soon, his secretary
told her chattily. She introduced herself, fetched some
coffee and discussed the weather. Then,

'I think I should warn you, he's in a terrible mood.'

'I imagine he is,' Abby said drily, wondering why
Marlene watched her with such interest. She was like
another Helen, she thought irrelevantly.

The glass doors burst open and Cort strode in
frowning. He stopped short at sight of Abby who put
aside her coffee and stood up.

'I'd like to talk to you.'

'I'm busy.' He strode on.

'That's no reason to be so damned rude,' she said sharply to his back. Cort turned around, eyes glacial, and Abby gave him back a cold glare. He'd found out what he wanted last night, hadn't he? The news hadn't been good but surely he'd been prepared for that. 'It will take five minutes, no more, Cort.'

There was some minute change in his eyes at her use of his name.

'All right,' he grunted.

As Abby went into his office she heard Marlene remind her boss of his next appointment.

'Mr Conrad will be calling to introduce the new partner, Mr Castle——'

'Buzz me when they arrive, Marlene.'

The name caught Abby's attention. 'Castle', she thought—there was a name to match an awful day. Cort followed her in and shut the door. He stayed by it, hands on hips and a look of cold contempt on his face.

'Come to plead for your spy, Abby?'

'He wasn't my spy—not the way you say it.'

'What other way is there? He owed his loyalty to TITAN——' Cort stabbed a thumb at his chest, '—to *me*. If he blabbed to you that makes him *your* man.'

'It wasn't his fault, Cort.'

He went to sit at his desk, as steely a look in those light eyes as she'd ever seen.

'Ah. You persuaded him to talk, did you, Abby? Used your Amazon charm on him? You'd be safe enough doing that with someone like Donaldson. I don't suppose he scares you stiff.'

She reddened at the reference to the previous night.

'Don't be ridiculous, Cort,' she snapped. 'You act as if the whole thing was planned espionage. A.W.E. isn't exactly ASIO you know—we don't go around subverting employees to get the goods on companies.

Paul has worked part-time for me on and off for the past two years and it was pure chance that he ever mentioned a thing about the island. If you want to chastise someone you might try some of your executive staff who talked about it in the locker-room at the squash club. That's how Paul knew. Nobody told him it was a secret. And I didn't attach any significance to it at first but it crossed my mind that it was odd the project never seemed to make the papers. It was you who made me think TITAN was keeping it quiet. You reacted to that silly poster. You were so quick to conciliate and leave those trees.'

He leaned back in his chair, said nothing.

'But even then if you hadn't—chased me to find out what I knew I would probably have forgotten it.'

'You know why I chased you,' he said. 'But maybe you don't want to be honest about it. If you can convince yourself I was merely trying to pump you for information, then you can keep me safely at a distance.'

'You flatter yourself, Cort. I don't need an excuse to keep you at a distance.'

'I think you do. You want to run a mile from me but I haven't let you——' He looked reflectively at her, 'And I don't think I'm going to.'

Abby spun away, paced across to the window. Her heart was thudding like a bass drum. He wouldn't let her run——? Arrogant devil.

'You don't have to keep up your act, Cort—I've told you all I know and A.W.E. has been won over by your masterly performance at our meeting.'

'Them—but not you?'

'I'm naturally cynical having been your target.'

'Like I said, pursuing you was pleasure, not business, Abby.'

She flicked her tongue over her lips. 'You might

have been willing to mix a bit of both but it was mostly business.'

He swivelled his chair around, left it shuddering as he stood.

'And for the record, Cort, I don't go around corrupting young married men with pregnant wives,' she went on tautly. 'That isn't my scene.'

'Okay, okay—that was a bloody stupid thing to say. I apologise.'

'Does that mean you'll give Paul his job back?'

'No.'

'Cort, he has three children—soon it will be four. Will you make him suffer for a few careless words?'

'I don't want him back—but I might be persuaded to do a deal on a reference.' The light-blue eyes ran over her. 'What are you prepared to concede, Abby?'

'It's like that, is it?'

'Don't jump to conclusions. I haven't offered my terms yet——' He walked over to her, stopping a handshake away but even so, crowding her. His anger seemed to have dissipated and there was a certain ambivalence about him. Cort looked as big and tough as ever yet oddly hesitant now as if he had not quite made up his mind just what favour he would demand for Paul's future. And after last night that was not likely.

'I want you to see the island for yourself,' he said at last.

'See the——?' she exclaimed. 'But why?'

'Some workers' accommodation is built, construction of storage facilities is under way. You'll be given a tour, shown how the site will be treated and that should convince you that there is nothing more to our reticence over the resort than mere financial considerations.'

'There is no need for that, Cort,' she said drily.

'Even if I came up with something volatile like a threatened wildlife species on Paradise I would have trouble convincing A.W.E. that TITAN was anything but concerned, ethical and sympathetic to environmental issues. Not after Grady Hill.'

His face had abruptly hardened again.

'Maybe so. But I'm not underestimating your powers of persuasion. I want you to see Paradise so that you'll know there is no issue there for A.W.E. No negotiation, Abby. That's the deal. Do it and I'll let Donaldson resign gracefully and provide him with a testimonial. TITAN will bear the cost of your visit of course. The copter runs Fridays and Mondays. You can go this Friday—stay the weekend and be back in time for the television show next week.'

'And will I get back in time for that, Cort?' she queried.

'God, Abby, what do you think I am?' he said roughly. 'Of course you'll get back in time. I don't plan to maroon you up there.'

She was confused. This seemed an extreme reaction to what was, after all, a small danger for TITAN. Yet in one way it was logical. Quite possibly Cort had flown a number of people up to his island. Investors, bankers, architects. Why not an outspoken member of an environmental group? It was sound business sense. And there was nothing wrong with Cort's business sense.

'All right,' she said slowly, thinking of Paul's desperate face. 'I'll go on the understanding that you at least give Paul a good reference and consider reinstating him. When I get to the island will someone from the TITAN crew meet me?'

'Yes,' he clipped and advised her to take summer clothes and swimgear.

'And is that all I have to do to fulfil my part of the bargain, Cort?' she asked steadily. 'Visit the island?'

Cort's eyes flickered over her face.

'Anything else I want from you, Abby, you'll give me willingly or not at all,' he growled. For the life of her she couldn't move or find the words to quash the idea that there might be room for doubt. Her tongue moistened her lips again—an old habit that had been conquered years ago in the re-making of Abby Milburn—she felt that curious defencelessness that was linked with Cort. When he put his hand to her face she could not prevent the instinctive tilt of her head into his touch. It was encouragement enough for him. With a low groan he pulled her to him.

'God, when I saw you today I was fit to kill——' he muttered against her mouth. 'But now——' The words turned into a kiss, his arms crushed her and Abby could find no defences even now. She slid her arms around his sides—formidable muscles rippled beneath her hands . . . last night his skin had been bare against hers . . . her lips opened, shaped to his, desire zinged through her body, arching her against him . . . Cort McKay, she thought wildly—it's Cort McKay and he wants me but he may not care at all for me and I'm already half way to . . . no. That would be the final irony. She thrust a hand into his hair. But if by some miracle he *could* care for her, she would want to be a woman for him, a real woman. And if she couldn't . . . Abby pushed him away. He didn't let her go entirely, but held her near him, looking into her face. His hard mouth was parted, still sensual—his breathing flared his nostrils a fraction.

The intercom crackled with Marlene's voice.

'Mr McKay—Mr Conrad's here with Mr Simon Castle.'

Abby went rigid. Simon? It couldn't be, of course. Castle was a common enough name. So was Simon. Cort frowned at her reaction. With his arms around her he couldn't fail to notice the sudden increase in her tension. She cast a fugitive glance at the door.

'What is it?' he asked. 'Do you know Conrad?' She shook her head. 'Or did you jump a mile at Castle's name?'

'I must go.' She broke free and started for the door. Cort went after her, closed a hand about her wrist and went to his desk, flicked the intercom stop.

'Send them in, Marlene.'

Abby struggled to be free, desperate not to see Simon—if it was Simon—but when she raised her eyes and saw Cort's speculation she stood still. He let her go just as the door opened. Abby walked away while the introductions were performed between the three men. One glance had been enough. It was Simon. And somehow she had to carry off this extraordinary meeting with the man who was indirectly responsible for the iron control she was applying now, in the presence of the only man since to break it. In a way it was Simon's doing that she was here at all. The old Abigail would never have barged into Cort McKay's life.

Cort introduced her to the older man but Simon came and took her hands in delight. He was handsome still, his clean-cut face blurred a little with extra weight and his athletic figure a trifle thicker about the waist. His eyes were a guileless blue, his smile boyish. Abby wondered how she could ever have loved a man with such emptiness in his face.

'Abby—you look fabulous.'

'Hello, Simon.' Quickly she removed her fingers from his grasp.

'Quite a celebrity nowadays. I've been reading about you in the papers. To think how shy you used to be.' He turned to Cort and Mr Conrad. 'Abby and I are—old friends.'

'Careful, Simon—that admission might not be in your favour if you have to sue me on behalf of TITAN. I'm not a favourite of your client.'

She allowed herself a smile at his faint discomfort and took her leave before Cort spotted the answer to the question he had asked her last night. Who was he?

On the way out she stopped at Marlene's desk.

'I take it Mr Castle is the new man in TITAN's legal firm?'

'That's right. When he becomes a full partner it'll be Conrad, Chapman, Connors and Castle,' she said smiling. 'All Cs. If he gets to be a full partner, that is.'

'He will. Simon Castle always gets what he wants. He should be an asset to TITAN.'

She was able to give Paul some good news as a result of her visit to Cort. The young man didn't thank her for her intervention and she couldn't really blame him. Her own confused feelings about Cort had loosened her tongue and lost Paul his job and she accepted the blame. Abby went home that evening edgy and depressed. The ground was shifting under her feet and there was nothing she could do but hold on and hope she survived the quake. Seeing Simon again had been less upsetting than she expected. In fact she realised, had Cort not been there watching, it would have meant nothing. Nothing at all. It was last night and that scene today with Cort that gnawed at her.

Jerkily she went to answer the phone, half dreading, half hoping it would be him. But it was Simon.

'Abby darling. There was no chance to talk today.'

'I think we just about covered everything, Simon,' she said drily.

'—you know you looked fantastic. Did I tell you you looked fantastic?' There was a warm, sexy tone in his voice—Abby remembered it well. That was maybe the one thing Simon had in common with Cort—that voice that could send shivers up her spine. Simon's did nothing for her now except to remind her of being in love with love.

'I believe you mentioned it.'

'I'd like to see you—talk over old times.' There was a suggestive sound to that. Simon wasn't being very subtle.

'Your wife mightn't understand that——' There had been a plain gold band on his hand today.

'My wife and I already have that problem. We really only live together as an economic arrangement, you see?'

She did.

'Meeting you again today, Abby, made me realise how stupid I was to let you go all those years ago. I'd like to get to know you again——' his voice dropped intimately.

'Would you, Simon?' He seemed to have forgotten in what circumstances he had 'let her go'.

'Do you know we had a pretty good thing going for us—I wish——'

'Yes, Simon?' There was an ice edge to her voice as she thought of the unfortunate woman he had married, no doubt waiting at home while he chatted up other women. For there would have been other phone calls like this one, Abby guessed.

'I wish we could get together again.'

'That's not possible.'

'If you mean because I'm married—that's no problem. A divorce is almost inevitable. My wife, well—she's not—how can I put this——' There was a faint slurring of his consonants. Apparently Simon's fuller figure was in part due to his continued liking for liquor. '—she's not warm. You know what I mean? Some women are like that.'

Something exploded in Abby. The words had a familiar, hurtful ring to them.

'The trouble with a lot of "women like that", Simon, is their husbands.'

The line went silent. He had not had so much to drink that he failed to catch on.

'I was good enough for you.'

'You never were.'

She heard his indrawn breath. 'Well, isn't that just a lovely thing to say to your first lover, darling—who is the man who has made me pale by comparison? McKay perhaps? Is he a miracle worker in the bedroom as well as the boardroom?'

'I don't know. But it seems you're not.'

She was about to hang up when he almost snarled, 'You chilly bitch. You'll be sorry you said that.'

'I'm sorry already.'

And she was. The nasty exchange sent her to her bedroom where she burst into tears and wished for a shoulder to cry on—for arms to hold her and someone's fleeting, tender touch.

Helen was happy to run the shop alone on Friday and Monday. Eager in fact. She would have the displays and the diminishing fan mail to herself. Abby made her apologies for the A.W.E. meeting she would miss on Friday night. It was tempting to tell Iris Broome that she was, in fact, going to see the development that they didn't believe in. But she had jumped in before and regretted it and simply said that she was spending the weekend with a friend. Probably she would never mention Paradise to them again. Later when she was at home, assembling the clothes she would take with her to the island, Abby received a call she had long given up on. The elusive John Mansfield had returned and received her message.

'No,' he told her, 'I didn't do any work on Paradise

Island, but Harry Granard did a bit up there. He
didn't finish it though—he had to abandon it because
of ill health. He died a month or so after he came back.
His widow might be able to help you, Miss Milburn.'

He gave her the number and she dialled it
thoughtfully.

'He wasn't well when he went up there,' Mrs
Granard told her. 'But he was like a boy about his
work. He was very excited about one of the ground
birds . . . when he came back he collapsed and spent
his last months in hospital.'

Abby murmured her sympathy. 'And his papers,
Mrs Granard?'

'They went to TITAN who asked him to do a study
for them. Most of the island is National Park and the
authority has conducted their own studies of course.
Harry seemed convinced that they had wrongly listed
one of the birds. He thought it could be an entirely
new species peculiar to the island but he didn't have
time to study it fully . . .'

'Even if I came up with a threatened wildlife
species——' she'd said to Cort. No wonder he had
looked thunderous. She had stumbled on his problem.
In all likelihood TITAN intended to disturb the
island's ecology as little as possible. The fact that they
had a private study done seemed to indicate good
intentions. But a possible rare bird—that was
something that would attract attention if made public.
The kind of attention from groups like A.W.E. that
could cost TITAN time and money. Checking her
camera and film, Abby wondered why she wasn't
elated. It was vindication of her opinion. But her
zealousness seemed to have flown. She felt curiously
detached about it right now.

Halfway through her packing Martin called and
eyed the overnight bag with interest.

'Going away, Abby?'

'I was going to phone you. It's just for the weekend, Martin. To visit—an old schoolfriend.'

He nodded and to her relief asked no more questions about it. Popping a pellet of gum into his mouth he made some coffee. Over it he said casually:

'How's the TITAN affair going?'

Abby's coffee spilt in her saucer. 'Affair?' she said lightly. 'Well—no news is good news.' Her reference to the lack of Joel Hamilton's colourful articles brought a smile to Martin's face and he laughed over her readings of a few 'Dear Abby' letters put aside for him. But when he stood to leave he seemed deep in thought. She went to the door with him and he caught her to him, kissed her rather harder than usual.

'You know I'm really very fond of you, Abby,' he whispered, touched her cheek briefly, then left.

She thought of that again on Friday when she sat in TITAN's supply helicopter. And wondered why, on Wednesday night when she'd longed for a shoulder to cry on and a tender touch, Martin had not sprung to mind. Martin, who had been such a pleasant companion—generous, warm—an open book. Instead she had wished for a man whom she hardly knew. A man she couldn't quite trust, yet whose touch had reached beneath the armour she had built as painstakingly as the tiny organisms had built the coral reefs below. Sadly, she looked down at the translucent blues and aquas of the Whitsunday Passage. 'Had been'. She had thought of Martin in the past tense. In some small way at least Cort McKay had achieved his intention to replace him.

CHAPTER SIX

THEY passed over the Whitsunday Islands—jade crowns of drowned mountains that had once been part of the mainland—white gold rims of sand set in aquamarine. Patches of reef and rock showed dark; deep water glowed sapphire and emerald. The day was brilliant. A jewel, she thought smiling down at the Pacific lying peaceful as its name within the wall of the Great Barrier Reef that ran over two thousand kilometres and against which the ocean battered relentlessly. Inside the reef's protection the islands basked in the sun and the tranquil waters of the Great Lagoon. For the first time she thought that this trip might be a good thing. A weekend on a tropical island—even with a TITAN guide—couldn't be all bad.

At last the pilot pointed to a tiny, densely foliaged island. She saw a broad strip of dazzling white-gold between two curving headlands and on the other side of the island a horseshoe beach—like a golden bite from the fuzzed green land. One high mountain peak rose in a solid mass of viridian near the island's centre. The copter banked to descend over a cleared area where Abby could see a four-wheel-drive vehicle waiting. As they landed she could make out two men lounging in the seat, wearing sunglasses and hats. One of them hoisted a bag from the back of the car and got out—clearly a passenger for the return trip. One of the crew off shift, she supposed as she gathered up her handbag and stepped down with the pilot's assistance to hurry, bent over, out of the radius of the chopper blades. The pilot followed with her holdall,

waved a hand to the two men then went back to
unload the supplies while his passenger boarded. Abby
turned to greet the TITAN guide sent to meet her.

She blinked at the massive figure getting out of the
vehicle, blinked again in case the sun's glare had
affected her vision. Cort—here?

'Hello, Abby. Have a pleasant trip?' He removed the
bag from her hand and stowed it on top of the supplies
packed in by the pilot. The helicopter rose from the
pad. Abby watched it go with a rather helpless feeling.
Cort lifted a hand to farewell the pilot and passenger,
then looked at her.

'You didn't say you'd be here,' she said through a
dry throat. The straw hat, ragged around the edges,
gave him the look of a castaway with his shirt
unbuttoned over a bare chest, and faded denim
shorts. Castaway. In sudden consternation she looked
around for signs of life. The chopper's stutter faded.
There was no sound save that of the sea's gentle curl
on to the shore and the cries of sea birds. The deep
quiet was music in itself but Abby would have given a
lot to hear the horrendous beep of horns and squeal of
tyres that signified crowds.

Cort shrugged. 'Didn't I? Get in, Abby.'

'Who was that leaving?'

'My overseer. He had to go unexpectedly. A radio
message came through that his wife was ill.'

His weight rocked the car and she got in beside him,
tension tying her straight-backed to the seat. There
was no getting away from here until Monday. Another
two days with Cort nearby. Two days and three
nights. She felt his eyes on her as the car bumped its
way down the mild slope from the landing pad.

'You'll see a temporary pier over there——' Cort
pointed and she looked but hardly saw the item in
question before trees blocked her view. 'That will be

rebuilt before the heavy work begins. We intend to build narrow roads all around the island and introduce a kind of golf buggy for the guests, and bicycles. No cars, except for a couple of 4WDs to patrol the beaches and transfer supplies. So far the road is only a track from the landing pad to the first phase of the crew accommodation, over to the jetty and down to the resort site. You look great, Abby.'

He tacked on the compliment in the same tone, making no distinction between his resort plans and her appearance. Perhaps that was an even greater compliment.

'Thanks. You look—different,' she said drily and he laughed.

'Want to see the resort now or are you in a hurry to get settled in?'

'The site please.'

They emerged from the trees and Abby caught her breath. She touched Cort's arm.

'Can you stop here?'

When he pulled up she got out, wobbling a bit in her heels. The sun was warm—much too warm to be wearing slacks and a jacket. Eyes panning from north to south, she removed her blazer, threw it over the back of the car seat and slammed the door shut.

A wide, wide beach shimmered below them— fringed by she-oaks and palms and lapped at by golden rippled shallows that shelved away into aqua depths. The ocean stretched to a brilliant blue-green horizon.

'Perfect,' she breathed and lifted her head to feel the sun full on her face. A rich, earthy smell reached her from the bushland, a clean, salt tang from the sea. The city and its chill and trauma seemed a bad dream. Abby breathed deeply of the warming peace and wished not to wake up for a long time.

She got back in the car. Cort smiled faintly as if he

was pleased at her reaction. He pointed as they headed down to the beach.

'The main resort buildings will go over there, and the pool——' he stopped as Abby put her hands over her ears.

'Don't tell me yet,' she implored. 'Let me see this first without imagining oiled bodies all over it and amplified music entertaining the drinkers by the pool.'

Nonplussed, he turned on to the sand and switched off the engine.

'I want to walk,' Abby said as she pulled off her shoes and rolled up the legs of her jeans. 'Though it seems sacrilege even to make footprints here.' Those blank, dark lenses stared at her and her cheeks flushed a little as she recalled their last meeting. But she looked out at the vast loneliness of the beach and its beauty clutched at her. Without waiting to see if he followed she leapt from the car, revelling in the feel of the sand beneath her bare feet. Childishly she looked back to see the marks she had made in the pale gold perfection. Cort was watching, hands hooked into the back waistband of his shorts. His shirt flapped aside revealing the matt of dark hair on his chest. He looked formidable even from this distance. Abby turned and walked on, postponing her misgivings in the immediate joy of the place. Once before she had been in the islands, stayed at Hayman and thought it breathtaking. But this—this really was Paradise. Longingly she looked at the sea and wished she was alone so that she could tear off her clothes and run into it.

A heady feeling came with the thought, as if she'd drunk too much wine. Softly at first she began to laugh. Uncaring that Cort watched, she skipped like a girl towards the water. When she reached the firm sand she began to run and the mild air rushed past her. Laughing again, she tried to pirouette but it had

been too long since school days and she ended up a
crumpled heap on the sand.

Cort's shadow fell across her and he reached down
to pull her to her feet.

'Are you feeling okay?' he grinned.

'Okay? I feel marvellous.'

'You look like a schoolgirl.'

'It's your island, Cort—it makes me feel like a
kid——' She looked at the slopes where his resort
would be built. 'I'm not going to think of it with
buildings and pools and umbrellas over there. Instead
I'll pretend you've built a thatched hut near the
tallest palm. With two steps—no, three steps down to
the ground . . . yes that, I can imagine. And I'd run
down those steps and across the beach every morning
without any——' She fell silent, cursing her brief
madness and waiting for his sarcastic comment. But he
said nothing and Abby's euphoria vanished as quickly
as it had come. Sedately she walked back to the car,
followed by Cort.

He took another rough track through lush greenery
and parked the car beside a sizeable pre-fabricated
house. Next to it was a partly built shed with odd
pieces of timber and tools lying around it. If this was
the extent of construction then the project was very
much an infant. But Abby was pleased to see it even
though there was no sign of the workers themselves.
She looked at her watch. It was mid-afternoon already.
The men were probably enjoying their tea break.

Cort carried her bag inside to a simple bedroom.
Polished wood floors, a small rug and stark white walls
that threw out a dazzling reflected light. An orange
and tan spread was thrown on the bed over which a
rolled mosquito net hung from a tester. At the window
a rattan blind was hoisted to reveal a matt of
casuarinas and aqua ocean glimpses.

'The bathroom is next to this room. Dinner is around seven, so if you want to shower and change now there will be time for a walk before dark.' He had removed the sunglasses and the hat and his light blue eyes moved quickly over her as she stood beside the bed. He pulled a folded paper from the pocket of his shirt and threw it down.

'I kept my side of the bargain,' he said and went out. It was a photocopy of a typed reference for Paul. Abby tossed it in her bag with a sigh. Quickly she unpacked her few things, stored them in the fitted wardrobe then showered. How quiet the island was, she thought as she put on a light pair of cotton trousers and a sleeveless knitted top. With her hair pulled up and knotted on top of her head, she wandered through the house but found no one. The sound of a handsaw started up and she followed it to the half-finished shed wondering if Cort intended to be her guide and if so, where he had gone.

Her footsteps faltered as she came upon him. Shirtless, he was cutting a piece of timber and though he glanced up at her, he kept on working. 'Construction is under way' he'd said. There was no one around.

Abby watched the motion of the saw blade, back and forth, biting deeper into the timber. She watched the sawdust spray and drop—followed one particle upwards as it passed through sunlight and vanished against a patch of jungle green. Stillness. A butterfly flashed white against green. Silence—just the lazy swish of the sea and the grate of the saw . . .

'Is there anyone else on the island, Cort?'

He straightened. The long tooth-edged saw blade quivered. His chest gleamed with perspiration, the muscles rippling as he breathed.

'No.'

Abby stared. Her pulses raced. Stuck here—with him. Alone. Virtual castaways until Monday. A thread of excitement entwined with her apprehension. Damn him! He stood there, looking like a Marlboro ad and having witnessed her tears and her craven wish to back off from him, probably expected her to be thrown into a flat spin at the prospect of a weekend with him. Cort watched her like a hawk, his remarkable eyes fixed on her wide, startled ones. Two days here with him . . . 'Anything else I want from you, you'll give me willingly——' Two days. '—or not at all.' And three nights.

'I see.' She stuck her hands on her hips and glared. 'Well, just don't expect me to do the cooking!'

He threw back his head and laughed. The sound was huge and hearty in the bushland hush—a sound that would be good to hear first thing in the morning, she'd once thought.

'When retreat is impossible, attack is the best defence. You're really something, Abby.'

She raised her chin. 'Did you arrange it like this, Cort? Surely you can get a woman to spend a weekend with you without stooping to subterfuge.'

He grinned. 'But you're no ordinary woman. And you aren't exactly spending the weekend with me in the traditional sense. Are you?'

'I'm here because you tricked me—blackmailed me into it, Cort. No other reason.'

His face darkened. 'I didn't plan for us to be alone. Some of the labour crew stay on at weekends—this time they all decided to go to the mainland. My overseer would have been here but he had to go to his wife. Sheer coincidence. But I was planning to come up anyway. You don't imagine I would send you here to lodge with a team of robust young men without protection?'

She stared at him. But now there was just him. And who would protect her against Cort McKay? She dragged her eyes from his dynamic form.

'If you want to continue working, I'll explore alone.'

He picked up his shirt and slipped it on.

'I'll come with you. How about a drink first?'

'Am I permitted to take photographs?' she asked as they drank fruit juice in the kitchen.

'Sure. Why not?'

She fetched her camera and hat. On the way out she saw a guitar standing in the corner of what appeared to be a living-room. It was the instrument he'd bought from her that night. So long ago it seemed since first he'd touched her.

'Which room is yours, Cort?' she asked casually.

'I'll show you later.' At her quick look he added, 'It's okay, Abby. I told you—what I want you'll give me willingly or not at all. I didn't get you here to seduce you.'

'No. You got me here to convert me.'

'That's right.' he drawled.

She waved her camera. 'Well then, Mr McKay, let's get on with my conversion.'

During their walk into the high, wooded area, she took a few snaps, but saw no ground birds that could be Dr Granard's find. At the island's highest point there was a three-hundred-and-sixty-degree view of its shores and of the ocean sheeting out marked by the islands to the south-west. In the late afternoon haze they looked like a distant school of whales lazing on the surface.

'You'll have to fence this off,' she said to Cort, moving back a pace from the edge of the exposed escarpment. Below, the wind had whipped the trees into tortuous shapes among pointed rocks.

'We will. But there's no danger if you're careful. I eat my lunch sitting there occasionally.' He pointed to the rock slab that projected over the hazards beneath. Abby felt a pang of alarm at the idea of him perched there, but moved away with apparent nonchalance.

'Your guests will want to climb up here with their cameras,' she said. 'What is the mountain called?'

'It isn't named.'

Wickedly she grinned at him. 'Call it Mount McKay.'

They both cooked dinner in the end. Abby tended the steak and Cort tossed together a salad and there was an odd intimacy in performing the domestic chores.

'Your mother would be pleased,' Abby commented, inclining her head at the healthy salad ingredients. 'Time off work and good food.'

'That's only two of Ma McKay's maxims,' he grinned.

She cast him an old fashioned look. He had changed into clean shorts and tee shirt before dinner. Neither left much to the imagination. The shirt clung to his chest, outlining its centurion curves—the shorts were white and brief on his athletic figure.

'Well, it's pretty clear you aren't hiding warm long johns under that outfit.'

He shook his head, addressed the salad in broad mimicry,

'Cort, my lad—you'll come down with a chill in your back, just mark my words———'

Abby gave a shout of laughter. 'She couldn't be that clucky—you wouldn't let her.'

'I'm exaggerating,' he admitted. 'My Mum's just great. One of the few women I know who are perfectly contented with their lives. She does all the traditional things—bakes for the local church bazaars, grows

vegetables and roses, knits—looks after my father——'
he glanced at her. 'Does that make you irate, Abby?
Such blatant satisfaction in doing things the liberated
ladies regard as drudgery?'

'Why should it? Your mother has chosen the life
and makes the most of it. That's fulfilment. But it
would be nice if those women who don't find enough
satisfaction in that role didn't have to be locked into it
just by virtue of their sex.'

'Is it why you haven't married, Abby?' Cort asked
when they sat down to eat.

'No. More likely for the same reasons you haven't
re-married.'

'You know about that?'

'I told you that I'd done my homework.'

'I didn't think my marital status formed part of your
research. So you know all the sordid details?'

'Hardly. Just the bare facts. In those situations I
don't imagine anyone knows all the details except the
couple involved.'

'True,' he said sardonically. 'And sometimes even
those involved don't see what's happening. I didn't.
Not until it was too late. My own fault,' he said to her
surprise. 'Kate and I married too young—my ambition
served to keep her in style but left her alone a lot. Kate
was one of your women who find no satisfaction in the
homemaker role, but neither did she have any
ambition to do anything else. It was bound to end in
trouble.' He gave a half laugh. 'Marriage is a mistake I
won't repeat.'

'What happened?'

'Kate found solace with a friend of mine—at least he
said he was a friend. They took off together with
Lindy.' His big hands played around the stem of his
wineglass. 'My daughter,' he explained, meeting her
eyes briefly. 'They left me a note. I found it when I

came home after a bloody awful day. A hundred-thousand-pound machine had been lost in a slide and one of my men injured. And I thought that was problem enough. Until the note.' He paused. 'That was in England. I made a new start over here after Kate's solicitor forced me to my knees to pay a divorce settlement. Lindy is twelve now. I haven't seen her for a year . . .'

No wonder he was tough, she thought. In one blow he lost his wife and daughter. And a friend. How he must have wanted to hit out at someone—or hold on to someone.

'Sorry for me, Abby?' he asked at the soft look in her eyes.

'You don't need sympathy now, Cort. You've done without and grown armour.'

'Like you.' His gaze held hers. 'But yours is thin and wearing down all the time.'

'And yours, Cort?'

He got up, took his plates to the sink, then came back to remove the empty wine bottle from the table.

'I'd grown accustomed to thinking it tougher than yours at any rate.'

'Tch, tch—are there chinks in your armour after all, Mr Mckay?' She followed him to the counter.

'Just the one,' he told her softly and reached out to touch her hair. She stood there, a plate in each hand as Cort drew his hand down her cheek in that amazing tenderness she associated with him. The remains of her armour began to shatter as she stared at him. Desperately she tried to gather up the pieces. He might not mean what she thought. That sweet touch of his might be just another of his talents. He might have lost out all those years ago, but he was a man who got what he wanted now. Wasn't she here because he'd demanded it—forced her?

Cort smiled at her confusion, leaned forward and

brushed his lips across hers. The scarce contact rocked through her body reviving desire and with it, apprehension. Abby knew in one flare of honesty that it was just a matter of time for her and Cort. She knew what he was—shrewd and tough and very likely still playing his games with her. But she would end up in his arms. Would give him what he wanted from her willingly.

Cort took the plates from her and nudged her towards the living-room.

'I'll wash up,' he said prosaically. Grateful for his retreat, Abby blinked the dazzle from her eyes. Now was too soon. She had to get used to the idea.

'Cort McKay—tough, resourceful boss of TITAN, washing dishes? What would the papers make of that?'

'What would they make of us being here together?' he grinned. 'Shall I tell Joel Hamilton and give him another chance at one of his fancy captions?'

'Titan and the Amazon in Paradise,' Abby quipped. 'Or how about—McKay and Milburn, marooned——'

But her amusement faded as she realised just what connotation Hamilton would put on this. He'd already created a sort of love/hate relationship for them. What a joke she would look if news of this got out. The fiery spokesperson of A.W.E. nipping off for a weekend with the man she'd been criticising. Abby glanced at Cort as he chuckled. His brawny lower arms were immersed in suds. He looked around.

'I won't tell if you won't,' he joked.

They had coffee in the spartan living room. Abby felt tense, keyed-up as an adolescent wondering if her first date would kiss her good night. From a pile of male magazines and trade journals she picked one and flicked through it just for something to keep her eyes from Cort who was leaning back, eyes closed. The picture of relaxation. Illogically she was irritated at his serenity that was so in contrast to her edginess.

'I've been in touch with Dr Granard's wife, Cort,' she said suddenly and Cort's eyes flew open. 'She told me that had he lived he would have done a study on a bird species here——'

He blinked a few times, ran a hand over his hair. Angrily he got up, looming over her.

'Leave it, Abby. I don't want to discuss it.'

'I could mention it on television next week.'

He took a deep breath. 'Naturally I hope you won't do that. There is no danger for any species here, TITAN will see to that and we'd prefer not to have to deal with an outcry from groups like A.W.E. But you'll have to do what your conscience tells you, Abby, and I'll—I'll have to do what I can to minimise the losses to TITAN.'

She didn't like the sound of that at all. The atmosphere grew thick. A giant moth blundered inside and fluttered about the lamp, its body hitting the shade with small, soft sounds. Outside insects hummed and the ocean, caught between the great outer reef and the continent, whispered against the island's shore.

It was a half-hour before he spoke again—a half-hour in which Abby skimmed through a half-dozen magazines that might as well have been blank.

'Play for me, Abby?' Cort fetched the guitar, pulled it from the cover. The strings were humming still as he walked over to the divan and held the instrument out to her.

'I'd rather hear you play,' she said. 'You did tell me you weren't just a pretty face.'

He gave a sheepish grin. 'I might have exaggerated.' Sitting on the edge of the settee, he clumsily fingered a basic chord, strumming stiffly with his right hand.

'Oh, give me a home——' he began to sing in a pseudo-American accent, stopping for long seconds while he re-arranged his fingers at each chord change. He finished and looked expectantly at Abby who had held in her mirth too long. She exploded in laughter, throwing back her head.

'You fraud, Cort McKay,' she gurgled.

'I didn't say I could play well—a little help with technique is all I need. How about one of those free lessons?'

'Now?'

'There's nothing else to do.' His light eyes teased. 'Is there?'

Abby licked her lips. 'It's difficult to teach with just one guitar.'

'You could stand behind me and guide my hands,' he suggested. 'I've always wanted to try a reversal of that old chauvinist image of the man teaching the curvy blonde to play golf.'

'Just one problem——' Abby said unsteadily, imagining wrapping her arms around him, 'I don't think my arms are long enough.'

'Ah well—I had to try. Just sit here beside me then, and tell me what I'm doing wrong.'

'You want to spend all weekend on it then?'

'Minx.' He went to his room and fetched a music book.

'Beatles music?' she said when he gave it to her. 'Are you a fan?'

'Who isn't then?' he said in a passable Ringo voice. 'The boys and me grew up at the same time—me being a bit younger, like.'

'You're crazy,' she laughed. 'Which number do you want to play tonight?'

'*Norwegian Wood*,' he said promptly. She raised her eyes to the ceiling.

'Oh the enthusiasm of the beginner—you realise that by rights you should spend a month perfecting Yankee Doodle or Camptown Races first?'

He shook his head. '*Norwegian Wood*, please.'

Tuning the guitar she said, 'Now this reminds me of a Dudley Moore-Peter Cook sketch——'

'—the Welsh piano teacher and the industrial tycoon who wanted to learn Beethoven's Fifth by Tuesday week.'

'That's the one—you like them?'

'Have all their tapes. There's one up here if you'd like to hear it later.'

'Maybe not—I have a feeling this lesson might offer all the comedy I could ask——'

'Is that any way to boost your student's confidence?' he said mournfully. Abby handed him the tuned guitar. He took it, covering her hands with his. For a second their eyes held and Abby felt a dancing rhythm inside her—and a lift to her heart that dispatched her fears for the moment. Withdrawing her hands she assumed the brisk tone of a teacher.

'Now Mr McKay, the first thing I'm going to teach you is an alternative G chord——'

An hour fled. Cort was like a big kid when his alternative G chord stopped sounding like a sick cat and more like music.

'This is beginning to sound like the song,' he said.

'You think so?'

'You play it for me then.'

She did so, embellishing the chords with a melody line and the faint sitar sound of the original recording. Cort sighed as she finished.

'All right, you win. How does Yankee Doodle go again——?'

Later, she played for him again. Her favourite pieces, some unplayed for years. The guitar notes had a new purity heard against the peace of the island. From her own student days she dredged up *Für Elise* and *Romance*, fused them into a Spanish piece then improvised her way through Duke Ellington's *Caravan*. Cort listened, head back, eyes closed. Thinking he had fallen asleep she stopped, but he opened his eyes and smiled.

'You're brilliant.'

Immense pleasure filled her at his praise. 'I'm not sure I should rely upon that opinion. As a musician you make a very good Chairman of the Board.'

'Cheek!' He leaned over and bunched his fist gently against her nose. Abby's smile fled at his sudden closeness; he studied her for a moment then stood up. 'How about a nightcap before you turn in?' He poured two cognacs, handed her one.

A breeze stirred the casuarinas bringing the sea's murmur close, swelling like an overture. Abby finished her drink with scant regard for the aged liqueur that demanded leisurely consumption.

'Good night, Cort,' she said, rising from the divan.

'Sleep well, Abby,' he said, not moving. 'I've got some work to do so I'll be up for some time yet.'

Her smile held relief. It was still too soon. She hadn't had time to get used to the idea yet. Cort saw the look in her eyes but his smile to her was warm.

She carried that warmth with her as she prepared for bed. In a plunge-necked night slip she threw back the bed covers, unrolled the netting and discovered a spider. The biggest, the hairiest spider she'd ever set eyes on. One shriek and she bolted to the door to collide with Cort.

'Ugh,' she shuddered and clutched his arm. 'A spider.'

'So I see.' His voice was amused and he looked down at her indulgently, his hands spanning her waist.

'I'm afraid of spiders.'

'So I gathered.'

Abby stepped away from him, smoothed down her

night dress as if she might somehow make it longer, less scanty. Cort put one hand on the door frame to balance himself while he took off one rope-soled shoe. Purposefully he advanced on the bed.

'What are you going to do?' Abby grabbed his arm again.

'Kill it.' He sounded surprised.

'Is it poisonous?' She looked at the hairy monster spread flat against the wall as if aware of its danger. She swallowed hard.

'No. But you're afraid of it, so I'll get rid of it.'

'It seems terrible to kill it just because I don't like the way it looks,' she shuddered. 'Could you—do you think you could just put it outside?'

Cort raised his eyes to the ceiling then directed a tender look at her.

'Of course. I forgot. We must conserve the wildlife, mustn't we?'

She retreated to the living-room while he fetched a paper bag and relocated the spider.

'Mission successful,' he said when he came back. 'Allow me to check your room just to be on the safe side. I don't want you shrieking like that in the middle of my sleep.'

An embarrassed flush crept over Abby's face.

'Even Amazons are afraid of something, Cort,' she said with dignity as he ostentatiously looked under the bed and in the wardrobe.

He came to where she stood by the door and looked down at her, a strange light in his eyes.

'I know.' Swiftly he bent and kissed her lips. 'Good night, sweetheart.'

The door closed and Abby listened to his footsteps down the hall before she slipped beneath the sheets. At her window the blind was up. Stars blinked, huge and white in a blue-black sky and the trembling tips of a casuarina swayed across the sickle moon. Love—she thought. I must be mad. Mad.

But she fell asleep with the peace of Paradise in her ears and a smile on her lips.

CHAPTER SEVEN

WHEN she woke in the morning, Cort had already breakfasted and was occupied outside. Through a window she saw him using a hammer on the timber frame, the exercise rippling every muscle on his broad back. His shirt was thrown over a stack of timber and he wore only faded blue denim shorts. What a beautiful man he was. Abby snatched her eyes from the window and went to eat breakfast in the kitchen and dwell on her new madness. Then she went outside.

The hammer whacked on wood, each blow echoing in the still air. Abby wondered why on earth he was labouring like this. According to the homework she had done on him, he had worked on site with his crews in the early days of his empire-building in England. But now he was at the helm of a huge business and the manual work was incongruous.

'You'll have another union strike on your hands if you're discovered doing this,' she said behind him. Cort turned around, looking her over in frank appreciation.

'Will you rat on me, Abby?'

She shook her head. 'Why are you doing it, Cort?'

'I like it,' he told her. 'The occasional bout of good, hard manual work stops me getting ulcers. And it keeps me in trim.' He laid one hand against the flat muscles of his stomach. Abby tried not to stare at his fantastic musculature.

'It works,' she said drily.

Grinning, he said, 'I'm thirty-six, Abby. I have to

work a bit harder nowadays to avoid middle-age spread.'

'Mmm. I can see that,' she nodded sympathetically. 'Those ancient muscles look to be on the edge of flab. Still, as you say—you are thirty-six.' Abby shook her head as if amazed that he was still able to stand upright.

'Minx. You should be more caring about a man's ego.'

Deliberately Abby inspected him, putting her head to one side and taking her time about it, in a reversal of the time-honoured masculine appraisal of a woman.

'You're not bad,' she nodded at length, 'now that I think about it—really for an oldie——'

Cort advanced on her, cutting short her play-acting. Laughing, she backed off.

'I was feeding your ego, you can't complain about that.' She turned tail, but he reached out and caught her shoulder then pulled her back against him with an arm about her waist. Her childish glee stopped the moment his arms slid warmly about her midriff. In the sundress she was wearing, her back was bare and making electric contact with the hard muscles of Cort's chest. He crooked his head to look down at her.

'Are you flirting with me, Abby?' he murmured. Abby felt his breath on her cheek, smelled the warm, masculine scent of him and closed her eyes.

'I think I am,' she whispered and his arms tightened as he laid his lips against the soft skin of her shoulder. It was the merest touch, then he let her go.

'Let's go for a swim.' He turned away and began clearing up the tools and scraps of his work. 'Go and change and bring your camera if you must. I'll be ready in a few minutes.'

Abby went inside and put on a bikini. In the mirror she eyed herself. It was written all over her face. She loved him. She wanted him. She should, she told herself, have a hundred fears about such a crazy situation. But only one nagged at her. Not that he did not love her. Stoically she accepted that Cort's flashes of tenderness could be simply a part of him, not prompted by her especially—but that he might find her less than a woman. It would be the acid test. If she found no fulfilment with Cort—him being the man he was and her feeling as she did about him—then she would know for sure that Simon's label was correct. It might be better not to know.

The Land Rover bumped over a track that climbed between the dappled grey trunks of poplar gums then fell down slopes of tussock grass spiked with ancient palm-like cycads and grass-trees. Into box scrub and then to the shore's palms and pandanus and casuarina. A bay curved away on both sides. Gold-shot shallows spread out for some distance before the water deepened to aquamarine. Even in the Whitsunday surfeit of beauty and colour this was a glorious place.

The water was mild and silky. Cort struck out for the deeper water but it was further than it looked and Abby gave up halfway. She lazily backstroked then turned to look through the thigh-deep, light-dappled water to see a few small striped fish flick away from her shadow. Eyes closed, she floated in the sun, hands idly paddling. Cort came up beside her, shaking back wet hair.

'What do you think of it?' he asked with a certain proprietorial air.

'Three stars,' she murmured. 'I'd give it four if you had some coral.'

He laughed. 'You didn't swim far enough.'

'You mean you have a reef?'

'A fringing reef. Most of the islands do——' he pointed to the deep water. 'Just out past the low-tide level. A poor relation to the outer reefs but fantastic all the same. Stay here, I've got some snorkelling gear in the car.'

He came back with masks and snorkels, adjusted the straps and handed her a set. They swam to deep water and slowly over the astounding sea garden. Purple staghorn coral bristled by cream and yellow leathery folds—green convolutions of brain coral juxtaposed by fanciful confections of pink and mauve. And the colours went on. A brilliant blue starfish. A motionless shoal of tiny fish hung like jewels then sheered away in one nervous, concerted retreat—a sea anemone convulsed in disco dress of hot pink spotted yellow, fringed with gently waving purple tentacles. There was a dreamlike quality to the submerged world. Abby had viewed coral reef before but from a boat with above-water sounds and other viewers' exclamations keeping it separate. Not like this—drifting in silence, temporarily part of it. Cort took her hand and she turned to see his masked face just beneath the surface. He pointed. A black Manta ray flapped into her line of vision. Abby jerked in surprise and the creature tore away like some hysterical old lady in a black cape. Cort's eyes crinkled behind his mask. Still holding her hand he turned her around and they went back the way they had come. In the shallows they stood and took off the snorkels. He smiled at her, said nothing. As she gazed back at the reef-shadows beneath the sea Abby said,

'You know I almost envy them . . . living in a world so quiet and beautiful . . .' She stopped, feeling foolish.

'That's how I often feel,' Cort draped an arm about her shoulder. 'But then I remember it isn't always like this. In the monsoon season reefs like this take a battering, and there's violence down there too. The big fish eat the little fish just as it happens up here.'

They waded through the sun-warmed water.

'The colours up here seem almost pale by comparison,' Abby murmured. Cort stopped and perforce she had to as well.

'Can't agree with that——' he said softly, taking a handful of her hair and holding up its dark, wet redness. 'I didn't see this colour down there——' he looked into her eyes. 'Nor that one.' Gently his arm curved around her, turning her to him. Her thighs touched his and they were suddenly close as if an electric current had run through their damp bodies, bonding them to each other. Cort kissed her and just for a moment Abby was back in that enchanted world of sweet silence and miraculous bursts of colour. He smiled, gave one last caress and a warm, salt flick of his tongue on her lips, then they waded to shore.

'Were you tempted to take anything, Abby—as a memento?' he asked, as she towelled her hair.

'You mean a piece of coral?' Abby said, looking up through wet strands of hair. 'Good lord, no. I don't know how people can be so greedy. Just to look is a privilege. Never take anything away and leave nothing behind—that's what I believe in. It would be a tragedy to find a piece of that purple staghorn coral fading on someone's mantelpiece—or to find a Coke can or a beer bottle back there——'

'Hmmm.' Cort leaned back, eyes screwed into slits against the sun. 'That's something that worries me——' he muttered, looking out at the deep water that hid the reef.

They stretched out on the warm sand, eyes closed, senses lulled by the whisper of the water and the faint cry of a heron or a gull. A breeze rustled the spiky leaves of the pandanus palms, stirred Abby's tangled hair. After a while she got up and took a photograph of the lush foreshore. With the camera sight still to her eye she panned across the sandy beach coming full circle until Cort filled the tiny rectangle. He lay on his back, lookng like some reclining Greek sculpture and she was tempted to include him on the film.

'What would the A.W.E. ladies say?' he drawled and she caught the gleam of lightning-blue eyes as he lifted his lids. 'They might think me the captive of the Amazon.'

Abby lowered the camera. 'They wouldn't make that mistake about Cortney Alexander McKay. You aren't the stuff captives are made of.'

'That's what I've always thought,' he said and rising, picked up his towel, threw hers over his shoulder as well. One large hand reached out for her as they walked back across the sand.

Over lunch Abby found herself giving details of her life she'd told very few, not even Martin who was a superb listener. Cort nodded his understanding of a childhood spent in competition with Zach for the attention of their parents.

'Zach sounds a trifle hard to take,' he commented.

'He's my brother,' she began stiffly, then shrugged. 'Yes, he has some rather superior ways but I love him just the same.'

'I would have liked a brother or sister,' he said. 'There are times when being an only child can be lonely.'

'Being a second, disappointing child can be lonely too. But I had a few good friends. Most of them have married and moved away. I wonder why it is that the very best friends move the longest distance away?' She shrugged. 'Being single of course, I don't have much in common with them now, but I keep in touch.'

'That brings me back to my question. Why haven't you married?'

'I guess I'm a career girl.'

'That's not an answer.'

'No, it's not.'

He laughed. 'That's put me in my place.'

During the afternoon they walked in a small pocket of rain-forest, the only one on the island.

'This won't be touched,' Cort told her. 'Apart from marking a proper walking track.'

Here the air was damp and rich with the smell of decaying leaves and wood. Vines, chasing the sun, looped and twined about the slim palm stems and the buttressed trunks of forest giants. Tree ferns, cunjevoi and crow's-nest grew to huge proportions on the cool, moist floor of the forest, vying with each other for their share of rain-water and space. It was a contest—a silent, ongoing competition for life—above where the trees raised their tops to sunlight and the orchids and elkhorns clung to trunks and branches for survival and below where every rock face, every tree trunk supported ferns, mosses, fungi in endless variety.

'Your island has everything, Cort,' she said as they emerged into open forest land again. 'How come it hasn't been developed before?'

'Not everything. There's a problem with the water supply which could prove costly to overcome. And being further out from the coast it makes the job of transporting people and supplies expensive. We dodn't have the topography for an airstrip like the one on Hamilton. Another company planned some development but decided it was too costly. I don't think so—not for my concept anyway."

She watched the faraway gleam in his eyes, the determined jut of his chin.

'Your dream, Cort?'

Slowly he turned to her and nodded. 'For the past five years since I saw this place I've been planning.

Three years it took me to get the land . . . it's been the only thing I've wanted——'

He didn't speak again on the way to the house and once there, he started work again on the shed, leaving Abby to her own devices until dark.

When he came to the kitchen, showered and shaved, Cort stared at the modest Formica-topped table transformed. Abby had found some mats and paper napkins among the spartan supplies, and polished some wine glasses. The smell of roast chicken came from the oven and Abby stood at the stove, a tea-towel tucked around her waist, presiding over the only available saucepan. Cort leaned a shoulder against the wall and let his eyes drift over the delightful picture she made. In a simple white halter dress Abby's skin, warmed to a richer tan by the sun, was smooth and flawless. Her russet hair was drawn up with gold slides at each side and cascaded in thick, gold-streaked waves to her shoulders. The pale drift of freckles across her nose had darkened a fraction, lending a girlish touch to her sophistication.

'I thought you weren't going to do the cooking, Ms Milburn.'

'It's a fiendish plot to get you to tell me all, Mr McKay.'

'You mean your cooking is so good that I'll weaken and give you Dr Granard's papers?'

'No. You might hand them over though for a promise to cease my culinary efforts. I'm not an inspired cook.'

Laughing he took a bottle of wine from the refrigerator and uncorked it while he watched her serve the meal.

'This is good,' he told her when he had sampled everything on his plate. 'Maybe not inspired, but I won't beg you to stop cooking. In fact I'm quite

intrigued by the militant Ms Milburn, aproned and
tending the dinner.'

'In my proper place would you say?' she asked him
drily.

'No . . . I've never thought the kitchen your proper
place, Abby.'

Her colour heightened at his subtle emphasis. He
watched her with interest.

'That was almost a blush.'

'At twenty-six I can't manage the full bit.'

'You almost blushed in my office too I recall. When
I maligned your intuition.'

'You were disgustingly rude.'

'I know. And wrong.'

'Aha. You admit it.'

'Yes. I think your intuition is in excellent order.' He
put out a hand and covered hers. 'Isn't it, Abby?'

Only a matter of time . . . Abby looked into his eyes
and knew that time was running out. Or just
beginning. She'd known long ago . . .'

'Yes.'

The moment passed. Cort poured more wine. Their
time would come and there was no hurry. They drank,
eyes meeting, smiling, waiting.

'You were disgustingly rude too,' he said after a
while.

'Not as rotten as you.'

He reflected. 'No—not as rotten as me. But pretty
damned awful.'

'What did I say?'

'Wounded me, you did.'

'What did I say, for heaven's sake?'

'That my big, strong shoulders didn't impress you.
A man can't take too much of that sort of thing.'

She laughed. Cort's eyes were fixed on her as if he
couldn't tear them away. His face sobered.

'Who was he, Abby?' he asked and her laughter died. 'Was it Castle?'

The fugitive look was in her eyes. 'Simon?'

'Don't try to tell me you were just good friends. I picked up a hell of a lot of vibrations in my office that day.'

'I was only twenty and I thought I was madly in love with him—the way you do when you're twenty.' She shrugged, tried to keep it light. 'I thought we were going to be married too, but I was wrong on both counts.'

'You had an affair.'

'Yes—or at least, he had an affair. I didn't think of it in those terms.'

'Was he the one who made you afraid?'

'Afraid, Cort?' she forced a smile. 'I'm no shrinking violet.'

'You've been backing off from me from the start. In your shop you turned into a one-woman band—stumbling over your stock to get away from me. It doesn't match the image of confident Abby Milburn. What did he do—force you?'

'Cort, I don't want to talk about it——'

'At your apartment that night, you called a halt when I knew you wanted me as much as I wanted you.' He leaned forward. 'Why, Abby?'

'I—didn't want to find that——'

'What?'

She was in an agony of embarrassment. 'Since Simon there has been no one. Not quite like that. I've never let anyone close because I couldn't bear to find out that he was right. He said I must be——'

'Frigid?' he exclaimed at her silence. Abby looked away, face suffused with colour, and after a moment was amazed to hear him laugh. Head back, he roared.

'Pardon me,' he said as she stared at him, 'but the idea is so ridiculous.'

Somewhere deep inside her an old chill turned to
warmth. How I love this man, she thought. At twenty
I knew nothing of love. 'I'm glad you think so,' she
said primly but her eyes were soft.

'I know so.' There was a deep husky note to his
voice. He lifted her hand and raised it to his lips. 'And
so will you, Abby.' He pulled her to her feet, laughing
at her gasp. 'Come and dance with me, love.'

Out into the living-room he whirled her, clasping hr
to him while he one-handedly inserted a cassette into
the stereo. Abby heard the music, moved her feet to its
beat but never did remember what it was. There was
too much to fill her mind, her sight, her heart. He held
her lightly away from him.

'I like you in white.'

'As a foil for my hair,' she reminded him of his
long-stemmed roses. 'Yellow too insipid, pink too
frivolous, red too full-blooded, I think you said.'

'Too full-blooded yet, I said in fact.'

'So you did. I didn't throw your roses out.'

'Good.' His eyes gleamed.

'Did you chase me to find out what I knew, Cort?'

'I thought so.' He chuckled. 'I told myself I was
pursuing you because of TITAN but I started
wanting you for myself the first night I came to see
you—when I took that guitar off the wall and wished
it was you I was holding.' The words were
murmured into her hair as he moved his head to the
curve of her neck and shoulder, pressing his mouth to
her skin. This was the music she would remember—it
hummed along her nerves, swelled as his mouth
touched hers and withdrew, touched again. Abby
opened her lips to his and kept him there, turning his
tender teasing to deep-breathed passion. Just for a
moment as his hands drove her against him and she
felt herself crushed by his strength she was seized by

the old panic. Immediately Cort's touch gentled. He curved an arm protectively around her and began to walk along the hall.

'Trust me, Abby,' he said and put his mouth to her temple.

'I do,' she whispered.

Dimly she saw that there were net curtains draped at the head of Cort's bed, that there was pale moonlight shafting in. She tensed again but he stopped with her by the window and tilted her chin for his kiss. Cort's hands trailed down, hollowing and spreading to the shape of her. Abby touched his face, felt at last the rough grain of his chin, the finer texture of his forehead. Her fingers ghosted downwards, pushed under his collar to trace his broad neck and the outward swell of his shoulders.

Outside the island held its breath. The casuarinas drooped in delicate brushstrokes—black against silver moonlight, silver against shadow. Over Cort's shoulder, Abby glimpsed it then closed her eyes as he released the tie of her dress and smoothed it from her in a sensuous sweep that drew one gasp from her, then another, as he slipped warm hands beneath her scrap of bikini lace and coaxed that too, to the floor. Her champagne mood on the beach the previous day was as nothing. Now the moonlight made a new madness, a silver burst of longing to know all there was to know of him. Fingers trembling she unfastened his shirt, pushed it aside and laid her mouth to the base of his neck. He smelled of lemons and wine and masculine musk. The touch of his bare skin on hers was electric—fusing all her feelings for him into one. She muttered something—some incoherent effort to tell him—and Cort put his mouth to hers, caressing her with words.

'We've only just begun,' he murmured and flicked

his tongue around her parted lips in a silken salute.
When he lifted her, Abby hardly noticed. Her head
was already whirling, her body already floating
somewhere in space. But she noticed when he put her
on his bed and pulled the net curtains around to
enclose her there—alone.

'Cort?' she whispered, her body warm and waiting
for him. His remaining clothes rustled to the floor and
he parted the netting to pull her against him. The
knowledge of his body against hers exploded inside
her, arching her to his hard-muscled warmth. Abby
ran her hands over his ribs, savoured the taut silk of
his skin, the smooth sweep of shoulder as he leaned
over her.

'Abby, you're beautiful,' he breathed and lowered
his head to her breasts. The broad, persuasive line of
his back sloped away under her fingers. His black head
blotted out the moonlight.

'So are you,' she whispered and his quick, surprised
laugh vibrated through her as he closed his mouth
strongly over her breast. And the quick pang of
pleasure grew as Cort's lips drifted to sun-gold skin
and pale . . .

'Cort?' she said, apprehensive when their time had
come. Her eyes flew open as his weight spread her
beneath him—but it was only a split second of
wondering for Cort's hard strength was hers and she
was wrapping her arms tight around him, drawing him
closer—closer——

Moonlight touched them with its still silver. Abby
stretched, smiled in wonder.

'What do you think now?' Cort asked softly.

'I think——' but the words gagged on a surge of
emotion and she turned her head to press her mouth
eloquently to his chest. His arm was around her and
he dropped a kiss on her tousled hair. With fingertips

she traced the superb lines of his torso. This man, so powerful, so vigorous—had offered her exquisite tenderness, had held back his own pleasure for her and only then let her know his strength. Her body was drifting, a delicious lethargy replacing the sharper joy of fulfilment. Contented, she nestled close to him, taking delight in this quiet intimacy. How I love him.

Under her hand, Cort's chest heaved and she lifted her head enquiringly at his rich, rumbling laugh.

'Frigid!' he chortled and drew her head down to kiss her.

Abby woke first, briefly puzzled by the net-draped strangeness until she remembered and turned to see Cort. He was lying on his stomach, head turned from her. The corner of the sheet was flung across his buttocks and Abby reached out idly to pull it away, curious to see all of him in this relaxed pose. His breathing was deep and regular. Abby moved closer to lightly run her index finger down his back and on to his thigh.

'Don't do that if you want an early breakfast,' Cort growled and she watched fascinated as his muscles stirred beneath the tanned skin. He flipped over, affording her this new daylight view of him which brought colour to her face. Cort grinned at her, eyeing her bare shoulders and breasts appreciatively.

'Do I pass muster?' he queried.

'You know the answer to that.'

He reached out for her, pulled her down to him. 'Tell me anyway.'

Abby lifted her head, threaded her fingers in his hair.

'I——' almost she said, 'I love you' but the words stayed in her throat. 'I told you last night, you're beautiful, isn't that enough?' Her tone was light, teasing, and a smile stayed on her mouth while she wondered how she could ever again be content with her life having known him like this.

'Beautiful!' he snorted and rolled so that he leaned over her. 'You need glasses.' Nuzzling her neck, he slid a hand to her breast. 'And I know what else you need——' She drew in her breath sharply as he tugged at her nipple . . .

'—breakfast.'

He got out of bed, pushed aside the net curtaining and put on a shave coat.

'Breakfast?' Abby's eyes were hazy.

'Breakfast.' He smiled a promise to her. 'But we've got the whole day, my love.'

As she showered and dressed, Abby wished the words were genuine. 'My love' . . . dreamily she dwelt on the pleasures of being his love in every sense, but brought herself up sharply. This weekend was a time in space. It might never be repeated, not like this. Once away from here Abby Milburn and Cort McKay would not be the same people. And this magic place would be gone too, buried under architect-designed piles of brick and timber, the sorcery of it smothered by the feather-bedding installed for its visitors. Abby sighed. The tourists would come and sip drinks in the resort bars, sunbake around the pool, dance until two in the morning to a 'name' band and go home to catalogue the delights of Paradise, never knowing that they hadn't sampled them at all. As she had. Paradise and Cort. Such a combination would never come again.

Sharing the tasks, they cooked breakfast together— eggs and bacon, toast and coffee.

'It must be this sea air,' Abby exclaimed as she finished. 'I rarely eat more than a piece of toast for breakfast.'

'Sea air?' Cort's brows rose quizzically and she ducked her head to her coffee. Chuckling he reached over and curved a hand to her nape, drawing her face to his. Across the plates and cups he kissed her then looked at her for long moments.

'Now I know how you look first thing in the morning,' he smiled, reminding her of his prophetic question. He had the answers now to all the questions he had asked her, Abby thought, feeling vulnerable. He knew almost all there was to know and had her love into the bargain. Somewhere in her warm contentment came a faint, chill breeze.

'Then you have no more questions for me to answer,' she said lightly.

'Just one more. But you might misconstrue it if I asked you now. Here's a simple one though—how about another swim?'

When she emerged from her bedroom in a bikini and wrap Abby carried her camera. It was a gesture of independence and that was all. In her heart she had already conceded the battle. Her conscience and the few unsubstantiated facts she had gathered were not enough to harass the man she loved. Cort's eyes went to the camera.

'It makes no difference, Cort,' she said, her chin high. 'Just because we—there's no reason for me to forget why I'm here.' She wanted to forget. Wished passionately that they had met in any other way. But Cort had taken her over so surely, so completely that Abby was afraid she might betray herself. These few shreds of Ms Milburn were all she had to hide behind now.

'I didn't make love to you to distract you, Abby. Take all the pictures you want.'

They walked outside and he handed her up into the 4WD.

'I'd prefer not to talk about A.W.E. or even the bloody resort for now. Let's have that swim and I'll pretend you're taking holiday snaps.'

She was taken aback by his vehemence. They drove down the track in silence and Abby decided that Cort, too, must want this 'lost weekend' atmosphere to prevail. Which was odd considering that he had brought her here to convince her that TITAN was a responsible giant. Was that why he had brought her here? Abby shot a glance at Cort's unrevealing profile. Perhaps last night he had achieved his goal by binding her to him as a lover. He would never know how successfully. When they left here she would tell him that he need not fear her meddling in his plans. She could give him that in return for his tenderness.

That set her mind a-ramble and her eyes were soft when the car stopped near the beach where she had skipped in champagne madness on Friday.

'If you look at me like that, my love, we may never make it to the sea,' he growled.

The euphoria began again and this time it was not entirely due to the empty drama of the shore. Heart racing, Abby slipped from her seat and looked as innocent as was possible in the circumstances. 'Why, Cort, I don't know what you mean.'

She took off her wrap and left it crumpled in a heap on the dry, white sand as Cort started towards her with a wicked gleam in his eyes. Though she fairly fled across the beach he caught her easily, bringing her down in a flying tackle that knocked the breath from her. He rolled her over and held her outspread arms to the sand as he lowered his considerable weight square on her. Abby squirmed under him, laughing and gasping simultaneously but falling silent as he kissed her, running his tongue around the curves of her mouth before tasting more deeply.

'Ugh, sand,' he said against her mouth.

'Serves you right.'

With a heave he pulled her to her feet, making a big

issue of dusting the sand from her shoulders, her back, her buttocks.

'Let's see how far you get this time, Abby,' he murmured and gave her a little push.

As she ran she cast him a knowing look. Held down by him she had felt his arousal and the chase was spiced with the certainty of its ending. A sudden sense of freedom made her look down in time to see the jade green bikini top slither to the sand. Panting, she remembered Cort's attentive hands sweeping sand from her skin. He must have untied the strings.

'Opportunist,' she accused and laughed as he caught her again from behind. Years of convention made her cover herself and she looked along the deserted shore as if gawking crowds might appear to witness her toplessness.

'There's no one to see,' Cort reminded her in amusement, 'but if it's modest coverage you want, allow me——' he pushed her arms aside and placed a large, square hand over each breast. Abby leaned back against him, warmed by the sun and fired by his touch. His shirt had been left behind on the sand and her skin tingled with the contact with his chest. One shoulder blade registered the steady pump of his heart. An audible sigh passed her lips—she watched the gentle swell of the sea through half-closed eyes as Cort's hands stroked and kneaded. Dizzily she was spun around in his arms. Cort knelt and touched his mouth to her bare breasts, curling his tongue about each nipple. She flung back her head and the sky swung crazily. His hands roamed over her hips and thighs, sliding under the narrow ties of the bikini. The scrap of green was clenched in one hand as he released her.

'You'll have to run faster this time, my love,' he breathed and let her go again.

That first day here she had wished she could run like this across the soft, white-gold sand. Modesty forgotten, Abby ran, revelling in the breeze that touched skin still alight with Cort's caress. Her ankles felt the change as she reached firm, damp sand and scattered silver drops of the translucent water that swirled lazily to meet her. Small droplets hit her back as the sea splashed up behind her and Abby made a last, laughing effort to evade her fate, but fell into the water Cort's captive.

'Did you ever see a film called *From Here to Eternity*?' he asked, sliding wet arms fast about her.

'I was too young,' she said smugly. 'I've only seen the television re-runs.'

'Minx—so have I,' he muttered in her ear and sank down with her to the tender caress of the Pacific and a tumult that had no connection with the ocean.

CHAPTER EIGHT

THE curving stretch of sand shimmered under a benign sun. Green foliage, dense and tipped with gold, hemmed in the pale strip against the ocean. Light flashed off the wind-screen of the Land Rover parked on the green verge and a scuffed trail led from it in a curiously meandering way across the sand. Along the path at intervals lay patches of colour, the last a small swatch of jade green alongside one of dark blue.

Tropic waters lapped about Cort and Abby. She pushed herself up on one elbow and looked across the beach, smiling at the ridiculous sight.

'Something funny?' Cort reached out a hand to her wet hair.

'We've littered the beach.' Her smile faded as she thought how one day it would be littered by others. Would Cort ever look out on this beautiful place and remember their crazy love game played here in isolation?

'Better pick them up, I suppose,' he said lazily, 'before the joyflight comes over again.'

Abby shot up, trying unsuccessfully to cover herself and look at the sky at the same time.

'Joyflight?

'A tourist thing they run from the mainland. It came over—oh, about fifteen minutes ago. Didn't you hear it?' Fifteen minutes! Her face flamed. Suspiciously she looked at him and saw his chest heaving.

'Cort—you rotter!' She flung a handful of wet sand at him and ran for her clothes. Even the mere mention

of being observed had reactivated her modesty.
Quickly she tied the strings of her bikini's lower half
while Cort adjusted his swimming briefs. They walked
slowly back to the car, picking up Abby's top and his
shirt on the way.

'If my thatched hut was over there near that tall
palm,' Abby said dreamily, 'we could stroll home,
climb the two steps——'

'Three,' Cort corrected, 'you changed it to three.'

She smiled. 'So I did. Then—we could go inside
and take a nap and later—we could go for another
swim——'

'Insatiable,' he whispered in her ear and helped her
on with her discarded wrap, his hands lingering on
her. Abby turned for a last look at this lovely place,
trying to imprint it on her memory—storing away the
delicate sounds and scent that a camera could not
capture. She would recall it always like this and never
come back to see it dotted with umbrellas and
imported Italian sun hats. So she would never see it
again.

Nor did she. Time which had dragged so slowly in
the years she would have preferred to skip altogether,
clocked up these memorable moments at an alarming
speed. Their interlude on the beach at Paradise was
already a thing of the past, Abby thought sadly, as she
looked down on the island from the helicopter the next
morning. The last hours of their stay at Paradise had
passed in companionable idleness as they explored its
beauty hand in hand, fending off the approaching chill
of departure with foolish jokes and banter. She had
played music for him again in the evening and they
had made music together that night in each other's
arms.

But now, though Cort's hand was strongly holding
hers, he was frowning and she could feel his tension.

He had been abrupt, almost rude to the pilot who had looked from him to Abby knowingly. Gradually she too sobered as the island shrank to a speck behind them. Cort made a phone call to his office at the airport while they waited for their south-bound flight.

'Business,' he said to her with one of his fantastic smiles.

Abby watched him walk away. So much for her motto—Take nothing away and leave nothing behind. She had no need for souvenirs of Paradise. She was taking away with her a hundred sun-drenched memories and she was leaving behind a part of herself . . .

Dave Sinclair was just leaving the office when Marlene put Cort's call through. His boss rattled off a couple of priorities for his attention and Dave grabbed a pen to jot them down. There was a very buoyant sound to Cort's voice today—Dave pursed his lips and listened, wondering if Marlene's tip was correct after all. Cort always felt good after a trip to the island but this time . . . this time Cort sounded as if he'd *really* been to Paradise. Well, well. He grinned from ear to ear.

'Are you listening to me, Dave?' Cort queried.

'Sure boss.' He read back his instructions and rang off. Still grinning he went to see Marlene, passing a man working in the spare office. He stopped and went back to the open door.

'Got everything you need, Castle?' The new junior partner seemed to fit the Conrad, Chapman & Connors image. Well fed, well read and eager to please their major client. The solicitor smiled, nodded and turned back to the pile of documents in front of him.

'It seems I could owe you an apology, Marlene old girl,' Dave said as he approached her desk. 'You remember your flash of feminine intuition that the

boss might be spending the weekend with—ahem—a
certain red-headed Amazon——?'

Marlene's mouth dropped open. Triumph lit her
eyes. 'I knew it! After she was here last Thursday I
told Charlie he might have to eat his words.'

'You mean Charlie didn't believe your educated
guesses either?'

'Pah! You men always underestimate us women.
Charlie even made me a little bet on it. "If those two
get together," he said—"I'll take you on that Pacific
cruise you're always on about."'

'Don't start planning your itinerary—I'm only
guessing that it was a tropical weekend with you-
know-who that's making him sound so different.'

'They're made for each other,' Marlene said with all
the fervour of the matchmaker. 'I knew it the day she
walked in here. And I'm not the only one. That
reporter picked up the vibrations too.' Marlene
pulled a face. 'Let's hope Hamilton doesn't get wind
of this—it would be a pity to see one of his crazy
captions on something that could be *real* important.'
She sighed, put her chin in her hand. 'Cort and Abby,
hmmmm . . . I've always fancied Fiji . . .'

Cort was a pleasant, polite companion during the
flight to Sydney. He could hardly be anything else,
Abby acknowledged. On an aircraft full of passengers
he could hardly be loverlike. Already they had
attracted attention just by virtue of their appearance.
But though he took her hand once or twice, her spirits
sank lower and lower with the plane. The wheels
touched down in Sydney and so did Abby.

Separate cabs might be advisable, Cort suggested.

'Of course,' she said coolly. She would be no
clinging lover. If Cort wanted to go on seeing her he
would have to say so. Within minutes Abby was
seated in a cab while the driver stowed her bag in

the boot. Cort leaned in before he shut the door on her.

'We have to talk in private, Abby. 'I——' his blue eyes were suddenly intense and he exclaimed in irritation, 'This is the wrong time, love. I'll phone you——'

Her spirits took off again, cautiously circling before climbing.

'Cort—about the television show——' she began but the driver had the motor running and Cort shut the door on her promise of silence about Paradise. At home Abby unpacked in a mood of cautious hope. Was it possible that Cort felt the way she did? She tossed her used clothes into the washing machine, caught back the white halter dress. How tenderly he had removed it from her that night—the same night during which he'd removed her fears. Dropping the dress into the tub she picked up the jade-green bikini. Had that been her, romping on a deserted beach? Perhaps it was all a dream and she hadn't really found a man who was companion, playmate and lover all in one magnificent package. And if that much was real, perhaps it was too much to ask that he loved her as well.

Apparently so. For he didn't phone. Abby went to bed and tossed and wondered if she was going to do what she'd vowed she never would—spend her days anxiously waiting a call from a man.

In the morning she fetched in the milk and the paper, almost expecting to find flowers or perfume outside her door. She made coffee, dropped a slice of bread in the toaster and thought of the breakfasts she'd cooked and eaten with Cort.

When the phone rang she ran to it. Her eyes were alight, her pulse racing, her ears attuned for a warm, masculine greeting. Her mother's voice was a cold douche.

'Have you no discretion at all, Abigail? I suppose you are old enough to go cavorting with men for the weekend but do you have to be so blatant about it?'

Abby opened and shut her mouth, her mind grappling with her mother's knowledge. Blatant?

'You realise of course,' her mother went on, 'that you have made yourself look a complete fool. Nobody is going to take you seriously when you criticise his company when its public knowledge that you've spent a weekend with him——but then I suppose he's clever enough to have planned it that way . . . the morning paper, Abby, page four if you want to see how small he has made you look——'

Abby hung up and went slowly to the table where the newspaper lay still rolled. She reached for it as if it was a cobra about to deal her a deadly blow.

Joel Hamilton had written in his same breezy style another instalment in the McKay-Milburn story. A small head photo of both her and Cort accompanied the article, arranged to appear as if they were looking at each other across the caption: TITAN'S WOMAN? A pain stabbed her chest.

Dynamic Chairman of TITAN Cort McKay has finally worn down the resistance of the lovely Abby Milburn, spokesperson for A.W.E. It seems that Mr McKay invited Ms Milburn to spend a long weekend with him in the tropics and the lady accepted. The pair are due to appear on opposite sides of a panel on the prime current affairs show on Wednesday. But perhaps one of them has been converted to the other's cause. Either way, sparks will fly . . .

There was more. A rehash of TITAN'S achievements and A.W.E.'s protests. A mild enough article— almost a gossip piece, reducing the island magic to a casual little affair.

'Shall I tell Hamilton and give him a chance at one of his fancy captions?' Cort had said. The pain sharpened. It was supposed to have been a joke. 'I won't tell if you won't.' He had smiled ... ah, that smile that ripped the heart from her. 'I'll have to do what I can to minimise the effect on TITAN.' His dream. He had to protect his precious dream. How successfully he had minimised her effect. She looked a complete fool now. The liberated woman, striding through a man's world but brought down to the level of a besotted teenager because of a love affair. Cort's reputation wouldn't suffer. 'The sly dog——' people would say admiringly. McKay the conqueror. While she would be a laughing stock. 'She went to argue conservation issues with him and ended up in his bed——' The A.W.E. wouldn't want her speaking for them any more. Against TITAN or anyone else.

And she didn't care about any of it—only that he'd done this to her. The irony was that Cort had already won her silence. Had he not closed the door of the cab so fast he would have known. Tears welled up—she kept them back, gulping to delay the sob that was gathering deep inside. Her eyes fixed on the picture of Cort. It was unflattering. But she had seen how that hard mouth could smile and tease—had seen his eyes lit with fun and affection and desire—had felt that tender touch of his lying in his arms in the afterglow ... her eyes widened.

He couldn't have arranged this. He *couldn't*. Not even to protect his burning passion for his island dream. It was too—too *small* for him. It could have been anyone. Someone on the plane. Of course—someone on the plane or even the chopper pilot who'd looked so interested in them—but the doubt remained. It was too convenient for TITAN—too timely. Abby took the paper to the phone.

'Say it wasn't——' she muttered as she dialled the phone number printed by the newspaper's name. 'Say it wasn't him——' After several connections and waits she got through to the newsroom.

'Joel Hamilton? Good God, if he was ever here this early in the morning I'd have the vapours, love—who wants him?' Abby tersely gave her name and demanded Hamilton's source for the story involving her. The voice became wary—lawsuit wary.

'You'll have to speak to him.'

After some negotiation he gave her Hamilton's home phone number.

'But he won't be capable yet, love——' he warned as she rung off.

Joel Hamilton didn't, indeed, sound capable. He mumbled and groaned.

'Abby Milburn? What the devil are you——'

'Who told you I'd been away with Cort McKay?'

'Mmmmph——?'

'Who, Mr Hamilton—someone from TITAN?'

The doorbell began to ring. Abby's eyes fixed on the door as Hamilton yawned and muttered, only some of his words coherent.

But enough.

'Rang from the TITAN office, said he was Cort McKay——'

Another yawn. '——that you and he'd been away together—yawn—thought it damned peculiar him telling me about it so I——'

She put the phone down. It made a dead sort of sound. The doorbell shrilled again. On its third ring she went to answer it.

Cort's bulk filled the door, his eyes sought hers anxiously as he moved towards her, a newspaper in his hand. His black hair was untidy. He needed a shave.

'Abby——' He put a hand to her waist as if he

would draw her close to him. She tore herself away, shaking with her tightly reined emotions.

'I can give you five minutes, Cort—I have to get ready to go to the shop.'

Cort frowned, thrust the door closed behind him. 'This article, Abby——' he shook the paper angrily. Beautifully done. Any minute now the northern accent would show up—see, I'm just a boy from the country—guileless, honest. Trust me.

'It really wasn't necessary you know,' she said coldly. 'I had no intention of mentioning your precious resort again. Yesterday I tried to tell you. After all, I owed you something for proving to me that I'm a woman after all.'

His black brows almost met. 'What the hell——?'

'I blame myself, Cort. All along I knew you were devoted to your Paradise project, and ruthless about it, but somehow I thought——' her voice shook a little but she steadied it, '—I thought you'd draw the line at this. Fool that I am I even defended you on television. "Cort McKay's not the man to hide behind anonymous letters——"' she mocked her own words.

He was still as a statue. 'You think I planted this story,' he said in a flat, abrasive voice.

'Not think. KNOW. Oh, at first I wasn't sure— you're such a superb actor that I thought Cort couldn't do this, not after——' she swallowed. 'So I checked with Joel Hamilton.'

'Did you really?' he grated between closed teeth.

'And now I'm wondering just what else you've done to protect your dream. Poor old Dr Granard—how very sad that he died just when he discovered something—but how convenient for Cort McKay!' The words spat out in fury, her restraint gone. She was hurting, weeping inside. His sudden pallor gave her some minute satisfaction—not nearly enough to

assuage the pain. With a fierce gesture he caught at
her arm, dropped the newspaper to hold her with both
hands.

'You can't believe that, Abby—listen to me——'

'Why did you come here, Cort—surely you aren't
still hoping for a lover's privileges after this? Perhaps
you are! You're just arrogant enough to think you can
play your war games and still have fun——'

'Damn you, Abby!' he ground out. 'How can you
even——' He shook her, glared into her eyes then
dragged her up to him and kissed her furiously,
swaying her head with the pressure of his mouth.
Even then she had to control her need to hold him, to
make his harsh mouth soften on hers the way she
remembered it. Island magic. When he let her go, she
put the back of her hand to her mouth. He still wanted
her—wasn't that just wonderful? But he'd had to make
a choice between his resort and her. Paradise had come
out number one.

'Finished?' she enquired coldly and looked at her
watch. 'You'll have to go, Cort. Your empire is
waiting. I do hope you enjoy it after the trouble you
took to protect it. There's a very unpleasant name for
a woman who makes love to a man for business reasons.
What *is* the male equivalent, I wonder?' He made a
sound like a wounded animal and his arm lashed back
as if he would strike her. For long seconds he stayed
like that, eyes locked on hers. Then he turned and
strode away. The door slammed behind him and Abby
let her tears overflow at last. Through them she looked
down at the jumble of newsprint Cort had left behind.
Uppermost Hamilton's caption mocked her—
TITAN'S WOMAN.

It was worse than Abby could have imagined. For a
few days work kept her busy. But the shop would
never be quite the same for her again. The echo of a

bass drum mocked her. Not the tearaway tempo of that night, but the slow thud, thud of today. And somewhere, sandwiched between the two extremes was locked a riot of rhythms against which Abby closed her ears. Or tried to.

The school holidays had finished and there was the usual back-to-school buying by students and teachers. She ignored their faintly curious stares but keenly felt the condemnation of the A.W.E. committee members who accepted her resignation icily and rejected her offer to make some public statement that might disassociate them from her personal life.

'Mr McKay has made several concessions lately and this—personal involvement of yours makes it all look rather—unsavoury,' Iris Broome said primly. 'Already there are some very crude jokes going around about it.'

'You're not suggesting that there was any manner of exchanged favours——'

'It's what other people say, Abby—and even in joke form it does our reputation no good. We'd prefer you to fade right out.' Iris would waste no time filling her place as spokesperson, Abby thought.

She didn't watch the television show. But Helen told her that the General Manager of TITAN took Cort's place on the panel.

Cort actually phoned her—once at home when she hung up and left the phone off the hook, and once in the shop when Helen was there.

'It's for you, Abby,' she said in a timid voice and held the receiver out to her.

'Abby, I want to talk to you,' Cort clipped before she could speak.

'There's nothing to say.' She thumped the phone down and kept her hand on it as if he might reach her through it otherwise. After a minute she stepped away from it and met her assistant's embarrassed, fascinated eyes. Helen, to put it in her own vernacular, didn't know where to put herself these days.

'If the same man phones, say I'm not here, please, Helen. You'd recognise the voice again, I dare say.'

'Oh yes, I'd know Mr McKay's voice anywhere.' She broke off and busied herself neatening the immaculate piles of catalogues under the counter. When the phone rang again minutes later Helen picked it up, went bright red as she looked Abby in the face and said, 'Oh—um—no, sorry. Abby—Miss Milburn is out—not here and won't be back until— won't be back at all today. Or tomorrow,' she added, gaining confidence at the end. She bit her lip when she hung up. 'Sorry, Abby—I'm a terrible liar.'

'All to the good, Helen. I'm sure he got the message,' Abby told her drily and patted her arm. 'Keep up the good work.'

Joel Hamilton phoned too. Under instructions Helen gave him the same spiel she'd given Cort. Abby got the feeling that her assistant was slowly piecing the whole thing together.

There was another spate of 'Dear Abby' letters prompted by Hamilton's article and her ironically timed appearance, representing A.W.E. in the women's magazine fashion pages. At any other time she might have gained some pleasure from the flattering photographs of herself in designer gear. But they were unable to revive her spirits. It was left to Helen to cautiously enthuse over them and to handle the mail. But the letters dwindled and in a week Abby gratefully acknowledged that she was old news.

Martin called around once more with reproach in his grey eyes.

'Have you got an ashtray?' he asked and at Abby's surprise added, 'My chewing gum lost its flavour. I needed something stronger when I read about your weekend with that old school friend.'

'I'm sorry Martin—I meant to phone you but I didn't know what I could say.'

Over coffee he looked at Abby's drawn face. 'Are you in love with him?'

'I—yes. But it isn't mutual.'

He took a deep inhalation of smoke, let it out then looked at the cigarette accusingly. 'Work—damn you. Work.'

'I'm sorry, Martin——' she began, near to tears that she had hurt this gentle man.

'Don't, Abby. It probably wouldn't have worked out for us anyway. I always felt I had to take it slowly with you. It was rotten timing on my part. I just—got overtaken by a fast driver.'

When he left he stubbed out the cigarette in disgust.

'No use at all,' he joked. 'Maybe if I tried bubble gum——'

'Oh, Martin——' She kissed his cheek but he pulled away.

'Let me know if you need me, Abby. I won't come unless you ask.'

A week later Cort phoned again at her apartment.

'Don't hang up on me, Abby, or I'll come over there and kick your door in to speak to you.'

'Very dramatic, Cort,' she snapped, knowing she should put the handset down right now. He was a cheating, calculating swine, she told herself. Her fingers played with the photograph she'd been staring at when he rang. She should have thrown the film away undeveloped.

'I've re-instated Paul Donaldson.'

'I know. Paul told me. Do you want a medal?' She looked at the picture. The day had been blue and gold, salt-tang in the air—a rustling breeze in the Pandanus palms—cries of heron and a gull——

'I shouldn't have let things go on like this—but God, you hurt me—let me see you alone so that I can tell you what I think——'

Hurt him? she thought. That's rich. 'I don't want to see you again.'

She dropped the phone in sudden, hurting fury and devoured the photograph again. Cort lay stretched out on the sand. The camera made him more than ever the Greek sculpture to which she had likened him that day. His hands were linked across the taut muscles of his stomach and his chest was silvered by the sun's glare. 'Captive of the Amazon' he'd said. It was almost funny. Abby didn't laugh as she tore it to pieces and dropped it in the waste-bin. With his perfume. He came to the flat. Abby didn't answer the door. Something about the ring of the doorbell warned her. How amazing. Cort could even put his stamp of individuality on the ring of a doorbell. From the window she watched him get into a big car—a BMW perhaps—and drive away.

For a while she was tempted to run. A long holiday wasn't out of the question. It was where, that was the problem. Just offhand there wasn't a place she could think of that would give her escape from Cort. So she stayed, alternately wishing she was in his arms again and hoping he was eaten up with guilt. He probably was, she consoled herself. Hence all the phone calls. Cort might be a ruthless devil, prepared to do whatever he could to protect his passion for his project, but nevertheless he had a conscience. One of his grey areas. It would nip at him until he could gather some crumb of forgiveness from her to still it—or until the end simply justified the means. His conscience wouldn't bother him once he presided at his first Paradise shareholders meeting. Abby Milburn would be a dim memory then—of potential trouble dealt with along with his union strikes.

The last week of September passed and Cort's conscience appeared to be already appeased. He no longer phoned her. Abby read a small item in the financial pages about TITAN. All good news. Contracts up—overheads down—'dynamic, resourceful chief executive Cort McKay predicts ...' Hoorah, she thought, and phoned Martin.

He didn't ask her much about it, seemed willing to take up his former role. They saw a movie, tried a new Chinese restaurant. There were tropical fish in a tank—jewels poised in the water ... she remembered a silent, beautiful world briefly shared with Cort. He had kissed her as they waded back to shore, warmed by a tropic sun, bonded damply together ... Martin asked her to stay the night with him. Gently she refused.

'All right. I can wait,' he told her and asked her to go to his club dinner with him.

'I didn't know you belonged to a club, Martin.'

'Had to wait to be asked to join this one. Finally made it last month. Very exclusive affair,' he told her with a grin. 'Run on old-fashioned lines. I have to smoke when I'm there. Chewing gum just isn't the thing, don't yer know.'

Helen thought it was such a good thing Abby was going out again.

'And Mr Salford is very nice. He doesn't mind about——' she bit her tongue and Abby ignored the slip, went on to tell her in rather too much detail about Martin's stuffy club and the annual tradition of ladies' night at a top hotel.

'I'll need to leave a bit earlier that day, Helen. Could you close up for me?'

Of course she could. And very likely do a quick re-shuffle of all the cabinets as well. Abby smiled, tried to give an enthusiastic description of the new dress bought for the occasion and pretend that it was a symbol of a return to normality. Not that she seemed to be fooling Helen. Over the next few days her assistant seemed more nervously attentive than ever.

But though it might not be a symbol, the dress looked fantastic. If she had lost a little weight that was all to the good, Abby thought as she turned before the mirror on the night of the club dinner. She looked less an Amazon. With a crooked smile she smoothed the amber fabric over her hips, ran one hand up to where it knotted silkily at her shoulder. Her other shoulder was bare and a gold collar marked the base of her neck. Stark simplicity from her hair—pulled back and French-plaited from crown to nape—to her amber sandals. But she knew she looked good. Her hair gleamed rich red-gold, the dress echoed the colour of her eyes and its fabric sheered away down her body in touch-me, touch-me-not flattery. It was pure glamour. And defiance. Abby Milburn, down but still fighting.

Martin gaped. Quite a few of the guests gaped. Abby Milburn's Statue of Liberty looks hadn't been quite forgotten yet.

'You could have chosen a less controversial partner for your first annual dinner,' she told him drily. Abby felt the eyes on her and sensed the whispers and drank three glasses of champagne beneath the chandeliers before dinner. And then she wished she'd saved two of the three.

For across the shiny dance floor she saw another member enter with his lady on his arm. The girl was petite, blonde, pretty. The man was six foot four, his dinner jacket precise across powerful shoulders, his frilled shirt pristine white over a deep, broad chest. His hair was jet black and his eyes were lightning blue.

CHAPTER NINE

'Do you want to leave, Abby?' Martin asked halfway through the dinner. She lifted her wineglass and smiled, keeping her head angled so that she would not see Cort and the girl with him.

'Of course not. I never fun from a right. Or do I mean run from a fight? Whatever.'

As the dinner was cleared away and the dancing began, Abby covertly studied Cort. In formal clothes he was distinguished. His hair gleamed dark—he'd had it cut recently, she saw, with an intimate recollection of driving her fingers into its shaggier length. Once he flicked a look at her from beneath dark brows and she turned away casually as if her eyes had lingered upon him by mistake. And in her mind she was hating him, touching him, loving him.

'Martin, ask me to dance.'

On the floor Martin held her as if she was a bundle of dynamite.

'People are staring.'

'Oh?'

'At you and McKay.'

'It doesn't bother me.'

'It bothers me,' he said abruptly and she reproached herself for not recognising Martin's position. 'Here I am with the most beautiful woman in the room and everyone knows that she's——'

'Titan's woman?' she supplied. 'If you want to leave, Martin, just say so. I'm sorry you've been embarrassed like this.'

'We'll have to stick it out another half-hour. The

President wants to talk to me,' he said shortly.

The President, whose wife was dancing, joined them at the table soon afterwards.

'Is your father a Kings old boy?' he started off and Abby stitched a remote smile to her face and let the old-school-tie recollections drift over her. The dancers slowed on the floor and she clenched her hand about her glass at the sight of Cort's blonde with someone. At least, she thought, she didn't have to watch her in *his* arms . . . her skin tingled a warning. As she stiffened in her chair a hand closed on her shoulder. A deep, arrogant voice spoke over her head.

'Evening, Hugh.' Cort shook hands with the President.

'Good to see you again, Cort—it's been too long.'

Cort said a curt 'Salford' with a nod of his head when the older man introduced Martin. The handshake was a mere token for both men.

'Don't let me interrupt. Abby and I will dance while you talk.' He grasped her arm, forcing her to put down her glass and rise to her feet. To onlookers his hold would look mere courtesy.

Short of kicking him in the shins there was no way she could avoid it. When they reached the floor, Cort put an arm around her waist and swamped her right hand in his. The mark of his fingers flamed on her arm. Heads turned in their direction and Abby glimpsed Martin watching as the President talked to him. Abby stared at a point over Cort's shoulder, blazingly conscious of him—the spread of his palm burning on the partly exposed skin of her back, the touch of his thighs—his warmth and the mellow, familiar scent of him that was in every breath she took. It made her remember . . . gold-streaked shallows and aqua sea swells and a gull-marked sky—'If you look at me like that, my love, we may never make it to the sea——' . . . my love . . . my love . . .

'You owe me a music lesson, Abby,' Cort said crisply.

Abby blinked a few times, shifted her eyes to his. 'You've got to be joking.'

'Do I look as if I'm bloody well joking?' he said roughly. 'I've tried to see you—phoned——'

'Conscience bothering you, Cort?'

'Conscience be damned,' he muttered and jerked her close. 'I haven't done anything to——' he broke off and exchanged a few conventional words of greeting with another man on the dance floor. But his abrupt courtesy did not dispose the other member to linger. Cort swept Abby in a tight circle, crushing her close in his arms, bending his head so that his cheek was laid against hers. She closed her eyes.

. . . a white-gold sweep of beach, fringed green with palms and casuarinas, lapped blue and green by the sea . . . footsteps on the sand in crazy, drunken patterns . . . 'you'll have to run faster this time, my love' . . . my love . . .

Abby's hand clenched into a fist at his shoulder, denying herself the delight of holding him, sliding her arms about his big, treacherous frame and letting him destroy her all over again.

'Maybe I should put your conscience at ease, Cort. After all it *was* a fun weekend even if you did use it——' Her breath jerked from her. Cort pressed her to him, his hand sliding upwards over her back.

. . . sand soft and sun-warmed, then damp and firm beneath her feet, droplets of water splashing up on to her back and the sun heating her as she dropped, Cort's captive, into the lace edged sea . . .

*   *   *

'Fun?' he repeated sharply and the nearby dancers looked over. 'Fun?' his voice dropped to a hoarse whisper. 'It was more than that, Abby—for both of us——'

'I love you' she had almost told him. She'd given him every other victory. Thankfully not that one too.

'Yes. I suppose in spite of everything I must thank you, Cort. If it hadn't been for you, I might have gone on thinking that I was——'

'Abby,' he growled and she fancied she heard pain in the sound. She was fancying too much altogether. The pain was hers. A killing pain that made the awful words spill out.

'It's made all the difference. Martin and I——'

Cort's muscles tautened. She felt the bunching of his shoulder beneath her hand. His arm locked her against his chest, squeezing her ribs. Her hand cracked in his.

'Cort,' she implored, white faced, 'you're hurting me.'

He let her go, took her elbow.

'Likewise,' she thought he said. In sharp, bitter silence they returned to the table. Cort nodded to the two men and was gone.

. . . '—did you ever see a film called *From Here to Eternity*——'

'How was the dinner?' Helen asked her eagerly on Monday.

'Just great.' Seeing Cort again had magnified the pain, emptied a bucket of tears on to her pillow later. Martin had filled an ashtray and made his second and final exit from her life.

'I might be a slow driver, but I see no point in parking in the middle of a freeway and waiting to be hit,' he'd said.

'Did you see—anyone——?' Helen went on vaguely but with an alert look about her. Abby cast her a startled glance.

'What do you mean?'

'Oh—you know—a club like that, you'd be bound to see people you knew——' her voice trailed away unconvincingly and Abby frowned. Helen took a deep breath.

'Abby—I've switched the Spanish guitar in the window for a Gibson electric. What with two English pop groups doing concerts this week, I thought it would be better.'

Abby's mouth dropped open. Then she laughed and patted her assistant's shoulder.

'Good for you, Helen. Do you know, I thought you'd *never* come out in the open. Now tell me, what else would you change?'

Helen bloomed. Became quite bossy in fact over the business of displays and Abby was content to let her take charge. Unable to unburden herself to anyone, she was pale and withdrawn much of the time and found herself unable to care whether the cornets or the trombones featured in the window. Helen watched her with troubled mouse-brown eyes and Abby did her best to convince her that all was well.

A few days later she took a call that raised her spirits. It was Zach. Trust her brother, spoiled-rotten Zach, to arrive back in the country unannounced.

'It's been five years, Abby. Can I come and see you tonight?' he asked. Same old Zach. 'I hear you've been in the news. The folks seem a bit stiff-necked about it. Want a shoulder to cry on?'

She almost cried right then and there. It wasn't quite the same old Zach after all. Since he'd been away he'd learned to read between the lines.

'You can stop casting those soulful looks at me, Helen. Tonight a tall, dark, gorgeous man is calling on me,' she began teasingly when Helen came back from lunch.

'Oh,' she clasped her hands together. 'You've made it up with him. I knew it. You and Mr McKay just *belong* to——' Abby stiffened to her full, regal height.

'It isn't Mr McKay, Helen. And I can't imagine why you should think so. Kindly don't mention him again. And,' she added coldly, 'I don't like the flutes where you've put them. When you get time, would you move them, please?'

'Zach, you look fantastic,' Abby exclaimed when she opened the door to her brother that night. At thirty he had finally discovered clothes that fitted. Five years ago he had still favoured cords and sweaters that hung in attractive shabbiness from his lean frame. Even their parents had found his clothes one small point of criticism though Zach's brain and achievements more than made up for it.

'You've found a man's boutique at last——' her gaze wandered up. 'And a hair stylist instead of a shearer. This new image must have improved your love life.'

He hugged her. 'I never had any trouble before. Now I just have more choice.' His faint acquired American accent twanged pleasantly.

'Arrogant devil,' she said.

'Truthful.'

He was, he confessed, not entirely in favour at home since he'd revealed the extent of his new commercial venture.

'Free enterprise instead of the Nobel Prize?' Abby asked drily and he laughed.

'It's quite a blow for them to find two shop-keeper in the family.'

'A research laboratory is still miles ahead of a musi shop in terms of prestige, Zachary,' Abby said i excellent imitation of their mother.

'Prestige or not, there is a definite cool win blowing. Could I stay a few nights with you, Abby until I find a flat?'

'Of course. How long are you staying? In Australia I mean.'

'Six weeks, maybe—I've some business to atten to.'

'Why do you need a flat, then? Stay with me unti you go back.'

A slow smile stretched his mouth. 'I met someone On the plane. She'll move in with me while I'm here.

'On the——!' Abby raised her brows. 'Just lik that?'.

'Just—like—that.' he said complacently. She stu died him. As arrogant as ever, she confirmed. H was handsome, more like their mother—and ha escaped Abby's red hair which was a legacy from their father. Dark brown hair, blue eyes, an inch over six feet and the build of a runner. Wid shoulders and a rangy body that looked good in hi casual, expensive clothes.

'Hmmm. Poor girl. You shouldn't be runnin around loose, Zach. When will you settle down an produce children? At least it would get Mother off *my* back.'

'I don't intend to marry,' he said quite seriously 'Life can give me all that I want without it.'

'Ha! I'll remind you of that one day,' she promised 'One day, there'll be a girl who won't move in with you just—like—that, and you'll be like a cat on ho bricks.'

'Not me.'

Later she did cry on his shoulder, metaphorically at any rate, even though Zach found it hard to understand why she had let herself become involved with a man past the point of no return.

'It just—happened, Zach. I knew from the start that Cort was ruthless and determined but it didn't help me any.' She looked at him sombrely. 'Haven't any of your girls become emotionally involved with you?'

'No. They know the score.'

She sighed at his masculine detachment. 'Well, so did I. You really are a superior devil, Zach.'

He agreed, and when he opened the door and brought in the suitcase he'd left outside, agreed with her too that he was presumptious.

Having Zach around was both pleasant and painful. It was fine to have someone to spill her feelings to, even if he didn't understand the half of it. But in some purely masculine ways he reminded her of Cort. One of her neighbours looked scandalised at her new flatmate and Abby decided that the truth would only make it worse and didn't explain. 'He's my brother' would sound like a well-worn cover-up.

The morning after Zach moved in Abby went to the shop, feeling a great deal more human than she'd done since Martin's club dinner. She was already regretting snapping at Helen and when her assistant arrived, throwing anxious, apologetic glances her way, she decided to put her out of her misery.

'About yesterday, Helen—I'm sorry I snapped. When you mentioned Cort McKay I'm afraid I rather lost my temper. The flutes are okay where they are.'

'Abby, that's all right. I never would have said it at all. It's just that I thought you——' she rushed on in a fluster, '—and from what he said I—just—thought——' She quailed under Abby's arrested gaze.

'From what he *said*? Have you spoken to him, Helen?'

'Well—um—oh, Abby, I'm a hopeless liar. He came into the shop one day and we talked and—I didn't mention it because it might have upset you.'

An old suspicion flared. 'One day before I went out with Martin to the dinner?' Abby remembered now. 'Did you see anyone?' Helen had asked about it, curiosity getting the better of prudence.

'And you told him I was going, I suppose.'

'He said he had to see you, Abby——'

Cort McKay probably belonged to a dozen clubs. How useful.

'That's enough, Helen,' her voice had never been so sharp, so cold. 'How dare you discuss me with him? You work here and I expect *some* loyalty. Perhaps you'd better think about another job at the end of the week.'

Helen shrank into her shell and stayed there. ABBY'S MUSIC was stiffly silent. Later Abby told her to move the flutes and re-arrange them, chiding herself for being petty even as she did it. At this rate, she thought in a grim sort of humour, the flutes would never find a suitable place. Her anger with Helen was a day-long thing. On her way home it occurred to her that Cort had felt the same when he'd found out Paul Donaldson had been talking about TITAN to her. It took the sting out of her fury and, exhausted by the unnatural day, she was relieved to sit down to an excellent dinner cooked by Zach.

'Unbelievable,' she said. 'You cook a steak better than I do.'

Zach quirked an eyebrow. 'Remembering your school cookery assignments I don't know that *that* is necessarily a compliment.'

'Good lord, you don't remember those lousy muffins and jam rolls!'

He grinned, touched a chip on a side tooth. 'Where do you think I got this, if not on your jam roll?'

She laughed. 'I'm not an inspired cook.'

Damn. Why did the most harmless statements have to revive images of Cort? She'd said that to him on the island, the first night he had made love to her ... 'Abby, you're beautiful——' ... 'So are you' ...

'You can wash up,' Zach told her as he finished. 'I have a date. She's calling here.'

'You whistle and they come running! Is this the girl on the plane?'

His lips twitched. 'No.'

'Hmmm. More free enterprise?'

Zach laughed as he went to the bathroom. He had only just turned the shower off when the bell rang once. She went to answer the door, smiling wryly. Zach not only got his lady friends to come running, but he kept them waiting as well.

This time she hadn't read the signature in the ring of the doorbell. It was a re-run of that other night. Only this time there was no lazy humour in Cort's face—and this time she didn't waste time with words before closing him out. Trying to close him out. His shoulder was wedged in the gap. The door edge hit him and he gave an involuntary grunt before he brought up both hands against the timber and sent her flying back. The door shut behind him.

'Such finesse—I thought you liked to be invited in,' she flung at him, trying not to stare at his black hair, the strong beautiful slopes of his chest. Cort was wearing grey trousers and a looped cotton sweater and a mantle of tension that bunched his big shoulders and drew his face into a ferocious frown. Abby stepped back.

'This is it, Abby. This time you'll listen to me or I'll break your lovely, stubborn neck.'

'Why should you want a hearing that badly, Cort? You éven roped my assistant into helping you. Why? Hoping to pick up where you left off—planning another weekend frolic up on Paradise before the bulldozers rip it apart? Take that fluffy little blonde with you. Give her a dose of the old McKay razzle-dazzle and she'll just melt in those big, manly arms.'

She backed away again, but he caught her and the big, manly arms yanked her to him, started her senses on a traitor's song.

'Let me go, you bully.' In desperation Abby brought up her hands, dug her nails into his shoulders. He grunted again, grasped her wrists and crossed her arms behind her.

'Will you *listen* to me?' he almost roared.

'It will be fascinating, I'm sure,' she panted, struggling to get away. Her writhings only forced her harder against him, her effort to kick him foiled when he forced her feet apart and planted one of his between them. Abby swallowed a rush of weakness, made herself stay still so that the solid strength of that thigh thrust between hers might be less evocative.

'Do you think if you tell me how you simply *had* to throw my reputation to the dogs to protect your precious resort, that I'll forgive you and say—of course I understand, Cort darling, please take me away again and——' There were tears on her lashes and a gulp stopped her.

'Abby, don't——' He released her arms to run his hands over her back. And it was worse, much worse. Because with a little more of that she might almost let him take her away again.

'Oh, don't kid yourself that you've shattered me. I told you last time, Cort. I'm grateful to you. That weekend proved very—therapeutic.'

There was a frozen silence. 'Therapeutic!' Cort

shook her and her hair flew about her face. 'You know as well as I do that it was a bloody bombshell. For both of us.'

Abby twisted away, not listening for fear she might weaken, speaking over him. 'Anyway, since then I've met someone.'

'Come on, Abby,' he said in disbelief. She looked beyond him, searching for something to hide behind. On the divan lay Zach's jacket.

'He moved in with me.'

'Liar,' Cort pulled her to him. 'You lied about Salford and you're lying now. There's no one else for you, Abby, and there won't be.'

No one else for me, she agreed despairingly as he kissed her. His mouth moved urgently on hers, his tongue on her lips and between. Her breath was rough and shaken, all her fine defences gone. Abby wrapped her arms around him, savouring the solid feel of him that had evaded her in dreams. His touch at her breast moved her restlessly in his arms. Bowing his head Cort kissed her neck, shaped a big hand beneath her breast then put his mouth against the full upper curve. Even through her clothes the sensation was electric. Calculating, ruthless swine, she thought desperately, and held him. I love you anyway. What am I going to do?

There was a hazard, triumphant gleam in his eyes as he raised his head.

'*Now*——' he said with emphasis, but softly, as one hand touched her hair in Cort's own tender gesture.

A door opened. The whistled strains of a pop song cut off part-way down the short corridor.

'Abby—where did you put my underpa——' Zach appeared, his discarded clothes bundled under one arm, a pink towel tucked about his waist. His hair was wet, flopping over one eye. A gold chain gleamed on his bare chest. He stopped, mouth open as Abby tore herself from Cort's arms. Cort bristled, a peculiar expression in his eyes, a cornered quality in the stance of his body.

'Who is he?' he growled on a rising note. Zach stiffened, his handsome face freezing into its arrogant mask. But he looked at Abby and remained silent.

'I told you, Cort, that someone had moved in with me. This is——' she cast a speaking look at Zach, '—Bill.'

Cort looked from her to 'Bill'. His hands clenched at his sides and his chest heaved under several deep breaths before he looked back at Abby.

'You won't want him for long, Abby.' The words seemed to cause him some disturbance for he swallowed, pressed his lips together a few times.

'Look——' Zach began. Cort put up a hand.

'Another word, loverboy, and I won't be responsible,' he said in a raw voice scarcely above a whisper. Then to Abby, 'I won't be back until I can prove you're wrong about me.'

The slam of the door rocked the apartment.

'So that is Cort McKay,' Zach said into the shocked silence. She nodded.

'For a moment there I thought he was going to hit me.' He put his hand thoughtfully to his jaw.

'Yes.' Abby's voice was small, shaking. 'So did I.'

'Now you see why I believe in free enterprise. It's a sad thing to see a man like that behaving like a cat on hot bricks.' At Abby's quick look he murmured, 'One of the big cats, of course.'

'You're wrong, Zach.'

'I don't think so.'

She paced around thinking, dredging up words and phrases to support her sudden hope. 'I won't be back until——'. Why come back at all if he felt nothing but

guilt—or desire? The first was no adequate motive and
the second could be easily assuaged. There would be
no shortage of women for Cort.

'Bill.' Zach shook his head. 'Couldn't you do better
than that? I ask you, do I look like a Bill?'

Abby gave a wan smile. He dropped his clothes on a
chair and came to her. And this time when she cried
on his shoulder it was the real thing.

Her eyes were still puffy when she went to work in the
morning. Helen came in and bit her lip when she saw
Abby's pale face but her 'good morning' was strained.

'Helen,' Abby began, 'I might have been a little
hasty yesterday. If you want to stay on here, I'd like
you to.'

'Oh, Abby,' her eyes filled with tears, 'I know I
shouldn't have gone behind your back, but he—well,
he looked so *sincere* and I always thought that you—
well——'

'Yes?'

'Had a soft spot for him.'

A soft spot, Abby thought painfully. Trust Helen to
find a description so pedestrian for something so
devastating.

'All right, Helen. I realise you thought you were
acting in my interests, so let's forget it.'

Helen was delighted to forget it, though with a few
glances of unrequited curiosity.

'And Abby—about those flutes——?'

'Damn the flutes, Helen. Put them anywhere you
like.'

So Helen was reinstated. Just as Cort had reinstated
Paul. Zach moved out and Abby tortured herself with
the idea that Cort might care for her after all. She let a
few days pass and then rang his office, not knowing
just what she could say to him. But Cort wasn't there,

Marlene told her and Abby quickly hung up before the woman recognised her voice. She found his home number and rang that. In amazment she realised that she didn't even know what his home was like. In love with a man and she knew no more about where he lived than that he had a Persian carpet and river views. But Cort didn't answer there either, no matter when she rang over the next weeks.

The city's trees were thick with summer canopies and the streets with lunch-time crowds and shoppers. Christmas was six weeks away and the pace of the city had quickened. It was hot and Abby sat down with her shopping on a shaded seat in Martin Place where she could see the massed colour of the flower stalls.

'I'd recognise that hair anywhere,' a male voice said behind her and she turned to see Joel Hamilton, untidy as ever, standing with his hands in his pockets. Undeterred by her deep freeze he slouched into the seat beside her and slid one arm along the back.

'A sight for sore eyes,' he grinned. 'I'm back on sports now.'

'It's a pity you were ever off sports.'

'Mad at me, Abby?'

'Shouldn't I be? Cort McKay lifts a finger and you print a story that makes me look a prize fool.'

'I wouldn't have written it if it wasn't true. Checked out the airline passenger lists to be certain first. I'm a reporter. You and Cort were news.' He shrugged. 'And he didn't give me the story, by the way.'

Abby stared. 'But you said—when I phoned you——'

Hamilton shook his head. 'I tried to ring you later but your assistant gave me the big heave-ho. It occurred to me that I mightn't have made myself clear. Played poker the night before,' he said in explanation. 'The call came from TITAN—through their switchboard—the man who spoke to me said he was Cort McKay—sounded a lot like him but it wasn't. There's that touch of Yorkshire or whatever in Cort's voice. It wasn't him.'

Oh yes. She'd heard that touch of the north—heard it vibrant and sexy and music to the ears . . .

'Then who?'

'No idea. But whoever it was sounded a bit hesitant—almost as if he'd picked up the phone on impulse, know what I mean? Not Cort's style.'

'If it sounded suspect why did you bother listening?'

'Honey—in this business it wouldn't matter if the lead came in from a camel driver in Arnhem Land—there's only one test it has to stand. Is it true? And I can think of some publications that don't even bother too much with that one.'

The flowers were bright in their tissue paper cornets thrust into buckets. A woman went by holding a bunch of carnations. Pigeons burbled on the grim metal cast of the cenotaph, perched irreverently on the sculpted head of the soldier. Abby watched them absently.

Cort could have got someone else to phone. But if so, why would he pretend to be him? Her brow creased then cleared. It didn't really matter who it was. What mattered was that it hadn't been Cort. She smiled, turned to meet Hamilton's interested gaze.

'You know, Mr Hamilton, you really should do something about your melodramatic style. Titan's Woman! Don't you think that was a bit too much?'

'Yeah, I suppose so. Couldn't resist an eyecatcher like that.' He smiled lopsidedly. 'Cort's a lucky devil. If I wasn't a poker-playing slob, too old to change my ways I might have tried to offer him some competition.' He leaned over and kissed her cheek. 'You'll have to write the last instalment of McKay v. Milburn yourself,' he said. 'I'm covering the Australian Open. Tennis will seem damned dull——' He got up. 'Bye, Abby.'

She watched him stroll away, hands in pockets.

Again she rang Cort's office. Again Marlene offered to take a message.

'No. It doesn't matter.'

'Isn't that——?' Marlene began and Abby hung up.

A day later she served a customer and struggled to recall the face when the woman said,

'Hello, Abby.'

'Don't you work for—Cort? Marlene, isn't it?'

'You remember,' she said with pleasure. 'Yes, I'm Cort's senior secretary. I need a recorder for my son Richard. He broke his at school, the little devil.'

Abby reached into the cabinet and brought out an instrument, laying it on the counter. Marlene looked around the shop.

'You've got some lovely guitars. That was a nice one you sold Cort.' She went on quickly as Abby stiffened, elaborating on just how nice Cort's guitar was.

'Did he play it for you?' Abby asked drily.

'No. *Can* he play?'

'In a fashion.' Abby thought of Cort, his big hands all thumbs on the guitar, trying to master *Norwegian Wood*. She proffered the recorder.

'Well, he'll have a bit of time to practise while he's away.'

'Away? Is he overseas?'

'Not unless you call Paradise overseas.'

'Oh. I suppose the resort is well under way now.' So

that was why he was always out. He was watching over his dream.

Marlene shook her head. 'No. That fell through. But Cort has some smaller project in hand now. I'm not sure just what.'

Abby frowned. The project—his dream? He would have fought like a tiger for it. 'It must have been a blow to him.'

Marlene took the recorder from Abby and looked it over.

'He was a bit difficult, I can tell you. Mind you, I've *never* seen him in a worse temper than he was over that last article about—er—you and him.'

'Oh?'

'Like a wounded lion. He wouldn't rest until he found out who gave the story to Hamilton. Have you got one of the plastic ones?'

Abby stared at her stupidly. 'What?'

'Recorders—plastic.' She waved the timber instrument in the air and Abby felt blindly in the cabinet and located a plastic one. Marlene took it.

'Hmm. Maybe this would be harder to break—what was I saying? Oh yes. It was my fault in a way. I was talking to Dave Sinclair about you and the boss and someone with a grudge overheard and must have decided to be nasty. Does this come with a case?'

She got no answer, just a blank look from Abby who was grappling with the flow of conversation, trying to sort out the bits she wanted to hear. Desperately she offered Marlene a cup of coffee which Helen made and brought to them. Mouse-brown eyes bright with interest, Helen then began to polish the items in the counter display nearby, while Marlene chattered on about Cort's terrible temper and how she hoped the break would improve his health. Dithery he was, she said sadly at Abby's surprise, and prone to making a lot of mistakes and even more prone to blaming it on others. Not himself at all.

'Charlie—my husband—says I'm a chronic worrier but sometimes I think it wasn't wise for Cort to go off up there alone. Of course the helicopter goes over on Fridays and Mondays.'

Alone—why was he up there alone?

'There's a radio,' Abby said.

Marlene smiled in resignation. 'Oh sure. And as I said to Dave Sinclair only yesterday—what possible use would the radio be unless he's beside it? Men!' she snorted in disgust. 'Just like big boys. Well, I ask you—if he got into trouble in the water, is he likely to have the radio with him? No, he shouldn't be alone in the state he's in.' She glanced at her watch and grimaced. 'I'll take the plastic one, Abby.'

Abby wrapped the recorder, her mind miles away in a tropic zone.

'By the way—that Mr Castle didn't make the grade after all.'

'Simon? What do you mean?'

'You know—as full partner in C.C. & C. He got the push from the firm for breaching client confidentiality. Cort was livid. He hit him, actually. Well, I must run. I have other shopping to do. Charlie's taking me on a Pacific cruise any time now . . . bye . . .'

CHAPTER TEN

ABBY'S dreams were fragmented that night as her mind prowled around Paradise in a poignant tour of its beauties and its dangers. Cort was there, tantalisingly out of sight but his voice caressed her . . . '—we've only just begun—you'll have to run faster this time, my love—call me the captive of the Amazon—a bloody bombshell for both of us——' And there was Simon's voice, too, alike yet lacking the warmth and depth of Cort's. 'You'll be sorry,' he said, and because it was not Simon she wanted to see, he was there, holding up a newspaper splashed with the headline she couldn't read but knew would say TITAN'S WOMAN. Frustrated, she searched for Cort—ran along the beach, dived down to the reef garden all silence and colour . . . 'If he got into trouble in the water is he likely to have the radio with him—he shouldn't be alone——'

'I eat my lunch sitting there——' Abby shot upright in bed, waking with the dream image of Cort falling, falling from the mountain on to rock pinnacles and tortured tree trunks far below.

The dreams made the decision for her. She had to go to the island. Once again she asked Helen to handle the shop in her absence.

'Of course, Abby. Are you going on holiday?' Her eyes rounded in comprehension at Abby's flush.

'I don't know how long I'll be away, Helen.' She avoided that excited, concerned gaze. Helen, she

thought, had found a new soap opera in the ups and
downs of her employer's life.

'That's all right,' she said with a sort of maternal
kindness, 'You stay away as long as you like, Abby.'
There was no doubt that she had overheard Marlene
yesterday and knew exactly where Abby was going.

'I might be back the same day.' Abby's heart
zoomed downwards at the thought. If Cort no longer
wanted to talk to her, she would have to take the
helicopter back immediately.

'Oh my dear, I do hope not.' Impulsively Helen put
her arm around Abby, standing on her toes to do so,
then scurried away to re-arrange the main window
display.

Zach called around as she packed a bag. So much
had happened since the last time she'd packed to go to
Paradise. It had been Martin who'd dropped in to see
her then, she recalled with a certain sadness.

'So you're going to give the poor guy a second chance,'
he said when she told him where she was going.

'That poor guy came close to flattening you,' she
retorted. 'But don't you males stick together!'

'Hang on——' Zach protested and did a little
shadow boxing, 'I can take care of myself, you know.
If there was any flattening to be done——' he
grimaced, raised his hand reminiscently until it was
fixed at Cort's approximate height, 'you're right. *He*
would have done it. Now, you will explain that I'm
your brother, won't you?' He pretended anxiety and
she gave a wry smile.

'I should never have let him think otherwise.'

'No, you shouldn't. But love turns nice, normal
people into lunatics. That's why I want none of it.'

'Your turn will come and I just hope I'm around to
see you join us lunatics.'

He grinned. 'Forewarned is forearmed. I've seen what

it's done to my independent, clever, talented sister.'

'Clever and talented? Ha. That was always your description, Zach.'

'And yours. Lord, I don't know how many times I had your musical ability quoted to me. "Your sister applies herself and she's four years younger than you." You must remember my reluctance for piano lessons.'

'I remember your piano lessons, not being quoted as an example to you.'

'Well, you were. The folks were always pretty proud of your musical talent.'

Not proud enough to come to her school concerts— not many of them anyway.

'They always criticised me, Zach—I can't ever remember them telling me I was good at something.'

Zach shrugged. 'They're an odd pair all right. But like I said—love makes lunatics of people. They're the quiet, clever kind—but lunatics just the same.'

Later Abby phoned her mother. The same old tension gripped her, the same and worse, coupled with the uncertainty about her trip tomorrow.

'Abigail,' her mother exclaimed, 'is something the matter?'

'How did you guess?'

'You rarely ever ring home, so I thought——'

Abby closed her eyes. It was true. She didn't phone. Her mother always did that every two weeks— sometimes more often. Regardless of her tight schedule she kept in touch and the calls that Abby took for granted—that often hurt her so—took on another aspect. Perhaps imperfect communication was better than none. Perhaps she would have to take a leaf from Zach's book and learn to read between the lines.

'I hope you're not mixed up in any more vulgar escapades——' Abby smiled. Reading between the lines wouldn't be easy.

'No vulgar escapades, Mother—just—mixed up.'

The helicopter pilot was a different one. He didn't seem at all surprised to see her. In fact he muttered something about Head Office warning them there could be a passenger but Abby could have misheard him as the rotor clattered overhead. The arc of white-gold beach was perfect, empty as they came in but a slight movement turned Abby's gaze back and she glimpsed someone near the palms. Someone with jet dark hair.

'Thank God,' she muttered in relief and clenched her hands. All those wild fears of injury and drowning had been unfounded.

'Could you wait for an hour?' she asked the pilot as he began unloading supplies.

'Forty-five minutes,' he offered, glancing at his watch. 'I've got a schedule to keep, Miss.'

So—forty-five minutes was all she had. Then she would know. 'If I'm not back then, go without me.'

The man grinned. 'Sure.'

Halfway down the track Abby took off her shoes and left them. The sun caught her as she emerged from the shade of an overhanging tree before she plunged into the shadow of the next. A butterfly flashed turquoise against the green of the tournefortias and Abby watched its progress, parallel with hers, with a burning, absent interest.

'What will I say to him?' The words hung echoing in her mind, unanswered, and she watched the graceful arcs of the insect with a sort of desperation. Her steps slowed as she saw through the thinning casuarinas to the wide, clean sands that had once sent her skipping carefree as a child and once—as a woman. At the thought her heartbeat quickened. Her throat felt dry and tense.

He might have given up on her by now. He might—

it occurred to her—have someone with him. The blonde that she'd urged him to bring. Abby stopped, pain filling her at the thought of him here with someone else. Other footsteps in the sand. Slowly she drew herself up to her full height and emerged from the casuarinas on to the beach. She would know soon. If he was alone. And if he loved her.

As far as his resort went, she thought, she was glad it had fallen through for the island's sake though she supposed Cort had not let his dream die completely. Whatever project he had decided to build instead would no doubt provide some compensation both financially and ... the salty air flicked up wisps of Abby's hair, flattening them across her face. She stopped walking, brushed it away. And stared at the building that nestled in the coconut grove.

'—I'll pretend you've built a thatched hut near that tall palm with two—no, three steps——' she had said to him. In her mind she'd seen it so clearly. A romantic dream. But here it was. Unbelieving she blinked, looked out at the ocean to rid herself of the shreds of fantasy. When she turned her head there would be just the empty beach and the hillside sloping back from the slim stems of the palms. Abby turned her head.

The whisper of the sea, the shrieks of terns and gulls came sharply to her—the heat from sun and sand prickled her skin and the tang of salt and overripe mangoes filled her nostrils. Every sense in her body awoke. The palm-thatched house was solid, real and her tears and laughter rose together. As she moved towards it a tall figure appeared, carrying a length of timber and a handsaw. With his back to her, Cort laid the beam across two supports and bent to cut it. Her pace quickened, quickened again until she was almost running.

She came right up to him, her feet making no sound on the sand or the spiky grass and goat's-foot creeper. For a moment more she hungrily watched him. He was shirtless, his skin almost mahogany and gleaming with his efforts. The long powerful lines of his back expanded and contracted. It was a time that would live on in her memory—the last moments she would spend alone—the last time she was on the outside looking in.

'Cort,' she said softly.

Cort whirled around so fast that he stumbled in the sandy earth.

'What——?' His mouth worked once or twice—his eyes opened wide in as vulnerable a look as she'd ever seen on him. Abby took a step forward, wanting to banish the expression. On a man like Cort it was unbearable. But the thick-lashed eyes narrowed. His black brows came swooping down. Cort scowled at the saw in his hand—turned his head slightly in the direction of the hut. There was a hint of bashfulness suppressed in the black countenance he turned on her. Abby swallowed down laughter and tears. Big, strong Cort McKay looked like a tough little lad who had been caught out building a cubby house for the girl next door. He had made a statement with his hut—a bold, powerful declaration that she couldn't miss. Cort's armour was all gone.

'So you finally decided to get off your high horse and talk to me,' he grated. He tossed down the saw and set his hands on his hips, glaring at her. If she didn't know, Abby thought, she might run a mile from this formidable, furious giant of a man. 'I wondered why the chopper hadn't taken off again.' He shifted his weight, folded his arms. 'In another week I was coming to get you.'

'To *get* me, Cort?' she raised her brows at the arrogant tone.

'One way or another,' he growled. 'How did you know I was here?'

'Marlene told me—she came to my shop to buy her son a recorder.'

'Hmmph. What did she say about me?'

Abby smiled, remembering now the determined drift of Marlene's chatter. She would have noticed had she not been so troubled. All those dire fears passed on so skilfully to make her come here. Marlene was a matchmaker. Someone from Head Office had even rung to warn the chopper service of an unscheduled passenger.

'She said you'd gone away because you needed the break—that you were indecisive, irritable, dithery.'

'Dithery!' Cort gave a snort of disgust.

'She also hinted that Simon Castle was the one who placed the story with Hamilton. Was it him?'

He nodded. There were shadows under his eyes, a deepening of the lines radiating from the corners. 'You hurt me,' she remembered him saying.

'I'm sorry, Cort, for thinking what I did—but I knew how important your resort was to you—and you even joked about telling the press about us being together—remember?'

He nodded again. Grimly.

'And—when I checked with Hamilton he said—or I thought he said—that it was you who'd phoned him. I misunderstood. The other day he told me the man had said he was you, even sounded a bit like you—but didn't have that bit of the north your posh school couldn't quite erase——'

He didn't smile. Abby desperately wanted to see a smile take the hurt from his face.

'What happened to make Castle so vindictive?' he asked roughly. What had he been imagining about her and Simon?

'He phoned me after that meeting in your office with some suggestion of us getting together again. I'm afraid I—might have insulted him. A touchy masculine subject.'

Eyes narrowed, Cort thought about it. 'A low blow perhaps.'

'Very low.'

'That explains it then,' he said and some of the hurt left his eyes. But only some. 'You kicked out your——' he held a tight rein on himself and spat out the word, '—friend, then?'

'Not exactly. Cort, he was——'

Cort held up his hands. 'For God's sake, Abby, spare me any of the details. It's bad enough imagining you with that smooth pin-up boy . . . I nearly knocked his teeth in when I saw him there in that bloody pink towel——' he gritted his teeth and looked so jealous, so frustrated that she laughed. Even thinking she had turned to someone else, Cort hadn't given up on her.

'By heaven Abby, I could——' he thundered and looked fit to strangle her.

'Cort, he was my brother.'

One succinct expletive rang out over the hushed sounds of the beach. 'Don't lay that on me, Abby—not that hoary old number.'

'Why should I come all this way to lie?' she asked with a touch of hauteur. 'It was Zach, my brother, and I told you his name was Bill so that you'd think—what you did think.'

His fists clenched and unclenched until finally a deep breath gusted from him.

'So there's no one. What about Salford?'

Abby shook her head. 'I'm afraid I lied—Martin was never more than a good friend. I'm sorry, Cort.'

'Sorry?' he roared. 'Is that all you can say? When

I've been lying awake at nights imagining you with someone else? Sorry?'

The palms rustled and their mauve shadows swayed. The shredded tip of a leaf flicked its shadow over Cort's face and the strip of a trunk angled across his torso.

'When I saw Joel Hamilton last week,' she said, studying the shadows on the sand, 'I told him how ridiculous it was to label me Titan's woman. I'm nothing of the kind.'

She looked up at Cort. He'd stiffened. There was uncertainty in every line of his big, beautiful body. Surely he didn't doubt that she loved him? She smiled, said softly——

'Now if he'd said *McKay's* woman——'

Cort moved with commendable speed, gathering her into his arms with a yearning that was evident in his patchy breathing and incoherent murmurs. His head buried in her hair and he held her tighter still, as if she might slip through his fingers.

'The first time I saw you I had this feeling——' he dropped a brief, fierce kiss on her lips. 'It must have been how Napoleon felt at Waterloo.'

She gave a shaky laugh. 'Oh no, Cort, as bad as that?'

'My God, yes. But I'd been nursing my baby along for years and had to keep fighting for the resort—kidding myself that I could ration my interest in you. What a daft notion! I should have sent Dave after you to find out if you were going to be trouble—I knew that was what I should have done, but no, not me—I kept thinking about a big, bossy redhead who looked frightened when I went too close.'

'You make me sound like an oversized mouse,' she objected.

'Mouse? Hell no—more like a tigress. But one afraid

of being trapped——' He stroked her hair with the backs of his fingers, delicately smoothing aside a few breeze-blown strands. 'That day when you came to my office to plead for Donaldson I was ready to write you off. I had actually told myself I wouldn't bother with you again—self-protection if you like—then I saw you and in a matter of minutes I wasn't thinking about the resort at all but wondering how I could find out what made you tick. Oh, I used Donaldson to get you here, I admit, and it was a rotten trick I suppose, but I knew I'd never get you to spend time with me willingly.'

'No, you were right. I was trying to ration my interest in you too. Without success.'

'I love you Abby. I wanted to tell you I cared for you while we were here but you kept bringing out that blasted camera and coming on with the A.W.E. spokesperson act and I thought you might think it was a ploy to distract you.'

She raised a brow. 'You'd already distracted me, Cort.'

'Besides——' he paused.

'Besides?'

'I was trying to come to terms with it myself. You weren't the only one who didn't want to be trapped. While we were here it was so good—so special—yet I suppose I tried to tell myself we just had a great affair going. I was tempted though to ask you to move in with me when we got back to Sydney.'

'Was that the question you thought I might misinterpret?'

'Hmmm.'

Abby's happiness dipped—a glissando of notes downwards.

'Then will you ask me now?'

He took a deep breath, looked mournfully into her

eyes and shook his head. 'Can't. Not unless you agree to one condition.'

'What's that?'

'Marry me first,' he said, then at her glowing silence, 'of course the sequence doesn't matter that much—move in with me then marry me if you like—our new accommodation is almost ready.' He glanced at the hut. 'Well?'

'Cort, you said you'd never marry again.'

'Changed my mind, didn't I?' His arms prompted her with a sudden squeeze. 'So—do you want me or not?' he demanded rather as he had during that very first meeting.

Music, Abby thought, feeling it start inside her. 'You big oaf——' she said in a voice that trembled. 'Do you think I came all this way to say no? Of course I want you. I love you—you crazy——'

'You're crying.'

Abby ducked her head to his shoulder. 'Don't be silly—of course I'm not.' But her tears fell on his warm skin and he felt them.

'It won't be *that* bad,' he consoled. 'I won't beat you—well, not often anyway. And you can keep your shop. I don't mind——'

Her head flung back. 'I can *keep* my shop! Well, isn't that big of you——' she began indignantly. But Cort's shoulders were shaking and she brushed the last tears away with her knuckles and started to laugh. Cort kissed her then, turning her laughter into eloquent murmurs in her throat. Palm shadows flickered as they drew back and smiled into each other's eyes.

'It will be good, Abby,' he said. 'I promise.'

'And I promise too.'

He groaned. 'What am I saying? Good? You're going to drive me insane! Every TITAN site will be a mass of trees and preserved old foundations——'

'That's the least of your worries. I intend to take over from your mother. Make you eat properly and work less.'

'And?' he grinned. 'There are three Ma McKay maxims, remember?'

'Do you think your mother would settle for two out of three?'

He laughed. 'When she meets you my mother will know I have everything I need.' A pause. 'And your parents—how will they react to me as a son-in-law?'

Abby hooked her hands behind his neck and considered.

'We-ll—do you think you might be able to make grandparents of them?'

His blue eyes crinkled almost to extinction. 'Is that my only path to approval?'

'Probably.'

His eyelids lowered languidly and his hands gently kneaded her buttocks. 'Then never fear—I shall do my duty.'

'I won't fear,' she promised, and kissed him.

'Cort,' she said huskily after a few moments, 'why did the resort plans fall through?'

He looked uncomfortable. Even sheepish.

'Hell—the problems with water were worse than we thought and with Keith Williams spending fifty million on Hamilton Island, condos going up on Hayman and Telfords putting millions more into South Molle, we did a re-appraisal. We always had an alternative site in mind. It'll go ahead one day.'

Abby stared. He was avoiding her eyes. 'Did you lose money over it?'

A grimace. 'Some. But what we've lost in money we'll gain in goodwill when we announce that TITAN will give its land to become part of the National Park—which means Paradise will remain wild. All except for this hut. The land it stands on is mine. Ours.' He looked down at her. 'Dr Granard's notes have gone to the University. His name will be given to any new bird catalogued.'

'You—gave it all up!' she said, stunned.

'Of course not——' he gruffed. 'What kind of a businessman do you think I am?'

'Not the kind I once thought,' Abby said. He'd given it up in a gesture as grand as his original plans.

Cort sighed. 'Oh all right. Take your victory. If you must know, once I'd looked at Paradise through your eyes, the resort didn't seem to fit after all. I kept imagining a Coke can rusting down on the reef. Anyway,' he added broodingly, 'how could I build a hotel here for cosseted, well-heeled tourists when the place is haunted?'

'Haunted?'

'Mmmm. There's this spectre of a naked woman that runs along the beach with red hair flying. Gorgeous. It's been bothering me for weeks.'

'Not frightened, were you, Cort?' she asked, running her hands provocatively over his chest.

'Terrified,' he admitted and opened the zipper of her dress. 'I thought she might never reappear in the flesh.'

The dress fell to the ground and his hands glided over her scantily clad curves. The clip of her bra fell apart under his touch. Cort shaped his hands to her breasts.

'Ah——' he sighed in deep satisfaction, '—so much more substantial than a spectre.'

'Have you something in mind, Cort?' she whispered, arms wrapped about his neck.

'I have. Something—*therapeutic*, darling.'

Laughing, she dodged out of reach, left the shade and ran on to the dazzling sands. A breeze played in her hair, touched her skin with cool, tender fingers and its champagne madness went to her head.

'Lunatics!' she shouted out to sea and as Cort captured her, her laughter rang out. He whirled her about and lifted her into his arms.

'I love you,' she nuzzled his ear. 'Where are you taking me?'

'To Paradise.'

'Boasting again!'

A beating noise intruded and a shadow raced across the beach. Abby and Cort looked up. The helicopter circled back towards the mainland but not before they had seen the pilot looking down at them.

'It'll be all over TITAN in a few hours,' Cort grinned. 'Marlene will get the shock of her life.' Abby laughed at that.

They reached the hut. The stairs weren't finished so Cort took a huge step up to the verandah.

'I hope you brought your guitar, love.'

'Guitar?' Abby's voice was soft, barely discernible over the ocean's lazy swish and the rustle of the palms.

'Because you still owe me another lesson.'

She laughed. 'I know that. Why do you think I'm here?'

Cort carried her inside and told her. To music.

Harlequin Presents

Coming Next Month

Available in October wherever paperback books are sold, or through Harlequin Reader Service:

In the U.S.
P.O. Box 1397
Buffalo, N.Y.
14240-1397

In Canada
P.O. Box 2800, Postal Station A
5170 Yonge Street
Willowdale, Ontario M2N 6J3

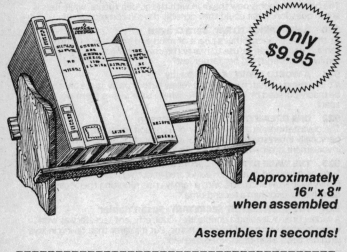

Could she find love as a mail-order bride?

MARIANNE WILLMAN

PIECES OF SKY

In the Arizona of 1873, Nora O'Shea is caught between life with a contemptuous, arrogant husband and her desperate love for Roger LeBeau, half-breed Comanche Indian scout and secret freedom fighter.

———————————————•———————————————